SOMEONE TO REPLACE HER!

Dear Christie:
Jana, Katie, Melanie, and I had a meeting of The Fabulous Five, only it wasn't really The Fabulous Five without you. We decided to ask Alexis Duvall if she'd like to hang out with us. Five friends seems like a better number than four, and besides, we don't want anyone to mistake us for Laura McCall and her Fantastic Foursome. Ha!

Christie's heart sank as she reread the part in Beth's letter about their asking Alexis to hang out with them. It sounded as if her best friends were doing very well without her. She hadn't *dreamed* they'd find someone to replace her in The Fabulous Five so quickly. And Beth's letter made it sound so easy. . . .

THE FABULOUS FIVE

Missing You

BETSY HAYNES

A BANTAM SKYLARK BOOK®
NEW YORK · TORONTO · LONDON · SYDNEY · AUCKLAND

RL 5, 009–012

MISSING YOU
A Bantam Skylark Book / August 1991

Bantam Books are published by Bantam Books, a division of Bantam Double-
day Dell Publishing Group, Inc. Its trademark, consisting of the words
"Bantam Books" and the portrayal of a rooster, is Registered in U.S. Patent
and Trademark Office and in other countries. Marca Registrada. Bantam
Books, 666 Fifth Avenue, New York, New York 10103.

PRINTED IN THE UNITED STATES OF AMERICA

OPM   0 9 8 7 6 5 4 3 2 1

Missing You

CHAPTER

1

Christie Winchell hitched her backpack higher onto her shoulder and followed her parents down the walkway into the airport terminal. Their plane had just landed at London's Gatwick Airport after an all-night flight from New York City. She was tired, and she ached from trying to sleep sitting up.

At the end of the corridor was a large room with a sign over the door that said CUSTOMS. Inside long lines of people led up to desks where uniformed officers were checking passports. The sight made Christie hesitate. She was actually in *London, England*! After weeks of worrying about leaving her friends and the town she had grown up in, she was surprised at the tiny thrill that ran through her.

"I think that line over there is shorter, Vince," said

Mrs. Winchell, pointing to the opposite side of the room. She was clutching the family's tickets, passports, and other papers.

"Right," said her father. Then he chuckled, and added as he led the way around the ends of the lines, "But don't forget, dear, in England they don't say 'line,' they say 'queue.'"

As they took their position and waited, Christie looked over the people standing nearby. There were a few people whose clothes made it obvious that they were from India and Africa, but the English looked just like Americans.

When it was their turn at the front of the line, Mrs. Winchell gave their passports to the officer, who thumbed through them quickly.

"You're here for an extended stay, I see."

"Yes," responded Mr. Winchell. "My company has transferred me to take over our London office. My family will be guests of your country for quite a while."

The conversation triggered a memory in Christie's mind of the day her father had announced they would be moving. He had said the new job was a *permanent position*. Ever since then, she had not liked the word *permanent* at all.

Christie had always assumed she would live in the town she was raised in forever. She had the best friends in the world there—Jana Morgan, Beth Barry, Katie Shannon, and Melanie Edwards. They called themselves The Fabulous Five and did everything together.

This year they had started seventh grade at Wakeman Junior High, and things were going great. She had even met a boy she really liked, named Chase Collins. Although she and Chase had had some problems, she still liked him a lot and hadn't wanted to say good-bye. Now she wondered if she and her friends would ever see each other again and if she'd ever even hear from Chase.

"Very good," said the customs officer, as she stamped their passports and handed them back. "I hope you enjoy your stay in England."

"I'm sure we will," said Mrs. Winchell.

Their next stop was the baggage claim area, where they retrieved their luggage from the carousel and loaded it onto a cart. Another customs agent waved them through the inspection area without making them open their suitcases.

As they entered the airport lobby, Christie saw a man holding a small white sign that said WINCHELL on it.

"Daddy, does that sign mean us?" asked Christie.

Her father looked around in surprise. "That's Finchley from the office. Good work, honey."

Finchley had gray hair and was dressed in a dark chauffeur's suit and cap. "I've got your motorcar outside, sir," he said to her father.

Christie was impressed by the way Finchley took charge of their luggage cart and snaked his way through the crowd to an exit. Outside he led them past a line of taxis, which looked like identical square black boxes, to a Mercedes-Benz automobile.

"You might want to take the dickey seat, young lady," Finchley suggested to Christie. "You'll be able to see more from there than if you sit between your father and mum."

Christie looked questioningly at her father.

"He means the folding seat, honey. Just pull it down."

Christie climbed into the car as the men put the luggage in the trunk.

As they drove out of the airport, a sign indicated the direction to Motorway M23. Christie looked out through the rain-streaked window of the car as they drove through rolling farmland. She saw several houses and barns with thatched roofs. A lot of the fields were green, but she was surprised at how many were bright yellow. She pointed it out to her father.

"The plant is called rape," he said. "The English make a lubricating oil from its seeds."

Christie thought about that. They had barely gotten to England, and already she had run into strange words, like *motorcar*, and *motorway*, and *dickey seat*, and calling her mother mum. And now the yellow plant called rape that grew all over the place.

Gradually, the infrequent farm buildings turned into small towns and then continuous rows of apartment buildings with narrow yards. She stared hard at the lace-covered windows, trying to imagine the insides of the homes.

Finally, they came to a sign that said RIVER THAMES. She remembered the lesson Mr. Dracovitch had had them do in the PEAK class—Pupils Excelling in Ability and Knowledge—about the Thames hundreds of years ago. Christie tried imagining what London had been like then.

As they drove through the downtown area, Christie was struck by the age of the buildings. There were very few gleaming glass boxes like the ones in America. There were also a lot more statues of men on horseback or standing in heroic poses. Strangest of all was the fact that all the cars were driving on the left side of the street. But that wasn't what worried Christie the most. What worried her most were the differences she couldn't see.

Finchley manipulated the car through the traffic, and before long pulled up in front of a red-brick building in a quiet neighborhood. The street was horseshoe-shaped and formed the three sides to a tiny green park. Christie giggled when she noticed the sign labeling it Queen's Pudding Square.

She took a deep breath and slowly looked up at what was to be her new home. It had two floors. A wide concrete stair with wrought-iron railings led up to a doorway set behind an arch. Both the first- and second-story windows on the right were bowed. It was not at all like the neat home with the large yard they were moving from. All of a sudden she felt very lonely.

"I'll get Mr. Dudley to help," said her father, as Finchley unloaded their luggage. He disappeared down a stairway that Christie hadn't noticed under the front steps.

Christie's mother gave her a smile of encouragement. "Why don't we go in?" She had that I-really-hope-you-like-it look.

The front door opened into a long hallway, and Christie drew in her breath. It was as if she had stepped back in time. All the rooms were to the right of the hall, and the first one was obviously the living room. The elegant furniture was upholstered in rich velvets and brocades, and the chairs and sofa were overstuffed and had high wingbacks.

Double doors opened into a dining room that had a long, formal-looking table centered under a twinkling crystal chandelier. Christie could just imagine elegantly dressed people having dinner there.

"Wow," she whispered. "I can't picture having one of our casual Winchell breakfasts in here. I'd be afraid I'd accidentally spill milk onto that table."

One thing that pleased her was that both the living room and the dining room had huge fireplaces. With the chilly drizzle falling outside, today would be a good time to have fires going.

As they walked from room to room, Christie had to bend her head back to look up at the ceilings. They were almost twice as high as the ones in the home they had left. The last room was a huge kitchen with cabinets so high, a ladder was needed to reach them and there was an island counter in the center of the room.

"I'll show you your bedroom," Christie's mother said, starting up a stairway at the far end of the hall.

Upstairs the room arrangement was the same. A long hall on the left side ran from the front to the back of the house. The bedrooms were on the right.

"There are three bedrooms, sweetheart. Yours is the one at the back, and ours is up front. Your father and I will use the middle room as a study. Why don't you take a look at yours?"

Christie hesitated outside the closed door. Until this moment it had been fun exploring the elegant old house. She had felt like a tourist or a temporary guest. But this was not a vacation. This was real. And she wasn't going to wake up and find it had all been a dream. Her mother had called this her room. *My room is back in America!* she wanted to shout. *And so are my friends and my school and everything else I care about!*

But I'm here, she thought sadly, and there's nothing I can do about it. With a sigh, she opened the door and stepped into the room. Instantly her eyes popped open. It looked like a scene from an old English movie. The bed was one of the largest she had ever seen. She almost needed a stool to get into it. And the mattress looked thick and soft enough to sink right through. Christie dropped her backpack and the plastic bag she had been carrying and walked around the room.

Against one wall was a large dresser. Across from the dresser was another enormous piece of furniture, nearly as high as the ceiling. It had drawers on one side and a door with a full-length mirror on the other.

"It's called a wardrobe," her mother said, entering from the hallway. "It takes the place of a closet, which these older homes don't have."

Christie opened the door of the wardrobe tentatively. It was huge inside and could easily hold everything she owned.

"The things that we shipped separately should be here in a few days," her mother went on. "Then you can arrange this room just the way you want it. I'm going to see if I can help your father and Finchley. Take your time getting used to it, honey. I'll be downstairs if you need me."

When her mother had gone, Christie went to the bed and pushed down on it. It was wonderfully soft, the kind of bed anyone would love to sink into at night—but it wasn't *her* bed. And how could she ever make this look like a teenager's room? Did she dare to tape her tennis posters up on the delicately flowered wallpaper?

"Who wants flowered wallpaper, anyway?" she murmured, burying her face in her hands.

After a moment she went to the window and looked out. Maybe there would be something encouraging there. But down below was just a small courtyard, hemmed in on four sides by buildings like the one she was in. Tiny porches covered with potted plants opened onto the court. An old lady wearing a raincoat was puttering in a small flower garden cramped into a narrow space between a porch and the wall of one building. A cat paraded around her, carrying its tail like a banner.

Tears welled up in Christie's eyes. This was so different from home. How would she ever get used to it?

Turning away from the window, she picked up her backpack and the plastic bag and slowly started pulling out stuffed bears. The first one was reddish-brown and was wearing a dress covered with hearts. "Melanie" was embroidered on it. Christie gave the bear a hug and placed it gently on the bed. The next bear was dressed in wild, neon-colored clothes and was wearing sunglasses. Christie smiled in spite of her tears and set "Beth" on the bed beside Melanie. The third bear had reddish hair just like Katie's and was dressed like an English judge, with a white wig on its head and a gavel in its paw. "Katie" was stitched across its robe, and Katie took her place of honor beside Beth. The last one was dark brown and was wearing a hat on which "Reporter" was written. It had "Jana" sewn on its shirt. Christie set the last bear on her bed, remembering how her friends had given them to her at the airport when she and her family were leaving. Had that been only yesterday?

Christie squinted through her tears at the four bears lined up against the large billowy pillows. Then she took out one last bear. This bear was dressed in a white tennis outfit. It had been her favorite for years.

She put it in the middle of the other animals and stepped back to look. It gave her a warm feeling to see the five bears together. She knew that even though they were far, far away, Jana, Katie, Melanie, and Beth were thinking about her at that very moment.

The thought of her friends put Christie into action. "I know what I'll do," she whispered. "I'll write them a letter. That will make them seem closer."

Digging through her backpack, she found a pen and some paper. Then she climbed onto the bed and settled in next to her bear friends.

Christie nibbled the end of the pen and thought for a moment before beginning. She wanted to tell The Fabulous Five how terribly lonely she was and how much she missed them. But maybe that would worry them too much. There really was nothing they could do from so far away. Of course it would be a lie to tell them she already loved London. But wasn't a lie okay sometimes if it kept someone else from feeling bad?

She worked her way a little deeper into the soft pillows and mattress and started her letter.

CHAPTER

2

Dear Everybody:

You won't believe how much I suffered on the flight over. I think my spine is permanently bent from trying to sleep sitting up.

You'll be happy to know, Katie, that some of the customs officers at the airport were women. Now we know for sure there are equal opportunities in England.

On the way in from the airport, I saw quaint thatched houses, and beautiful fields that were green and yellow. This is a gorgeous country.

You guys would go crazy over my room. It's on the second floor of our flat, and it has this humongous bed that you literally sink into up to your neck. I'm sitting on it at this very moment, and the mattress is so soft, I swear it must be made out of cotton candy.

Guess who's sitting with me? The bears you gave me, of course. Thank you very, very much. I love them.

Write real soon, and tell me about all the great things you guys have been doing. I'll write my next letter to another one of you. You can have fun guessing who the lucky person will be.
Love,
    Christie

"She sounds like she's having a great time," said Jana. It was Saturday afternoon, and The Fabulous Five minus Christie were sprawled around Jana's bedroom. Jana had just finished reading Christie's letter out loud. It had been mailed to her apartment.

"That bed of hers sounds fantastic!" said Beth. "I'd die for one like it."

"She didn't say whether she's met any boys yet," said Melanie. "I'm crazy about their English accents. I wonder if they call dating 'dating' in England."

"Probably," said Beth. "What else would they call it?"

"Who knows?" said Katie. "They call lawyers, 'solicitors.'"

"You'd know about that, since you want to be a lawyer." Jana laughed. "And if you were in England, you could wear one of those funny white wigs all the lawyers and judges wear."

"Gee," said Melanie, suddenly looking sad. "I miss Christie."

"Me, too," agreed Jana softly.

"Yeah," chimed in Katie. "Right now she ought to

be lying right here on Jana's bed with a book in her lap, half listening to what we're saying."

"I keep expecting her to come up to me in school," admitted Beth. "I even catch myself looking down the hallways for her."

"I can't wait until Christie moves back," said Melanie. Katie looked at her glumly. "If she ever does."

"Don't say that!" Beth responded sharply. Her eyes were watery.

"But it's true," said Jana. "She may not be back and The Fabulous Five will never be the same without her."

The room grew quiet, and the girls avoided looking at each other.

I miss Christie as badly as Beth does, Katie thought defensively. *She shouldn't get mad at me because I said what we all know. We may never, ever see Christie again except in pictures she sends us*. Katie squeezed her hands into tight little fists.

At the same time, Beth was thinking: *How does Katie know Christie won't be coming home soon, anyway? We shouldn't think that way. Her father got a big promotion, didn't he? Maybe he'll do such a great job, they'll give him another promotion, and then they'll come home. Or maybe he won't like the job, and he'll quit.*

I wish Katie and Beth wouldn't argue about Christie when she's not here, thought Melanie. *It makes me feel worse.* She gulped hard. *Besides, we ought to be happy that Christie's having such a good time, seeing the world.*

Jana looked at her hands, folded in her lap. *It's sure going to be different without Christie. Whenever one of the others got a wild idea, it was always good to know that Christie was around to help keep things straight. On top of that she was a lot of fun.* Jana sighed. *The Fabulous Five just isn't the same with her over there and us over here.*

Jana cleared her throat and looked at her friends. "Well, we can't just sit around moping. We have to decide how we're going to answer Christie's letter. Do we write her one big letter from all of us, or do we each write her a separate letter?"

"I think we ought to write her one big one," said Katie.

"And tell her about all the fun things we're doing. We don't want her to feel sorry for us because she's having a big adventure while we're stuck doing the same old boring stuff," agreed Melanie.

"Let's each write our own part," suggested Katie. "Then we can put them all in one envelope tomorrow and mail it."

"Good idea," said Jana. "And remember, we want Christie to know we miss her, but we don't want her to think The Fabulous Five is falling apart. Okay? Now let's get started."

"Wow!" said Dekeisha Adams. "It sounds as if Christie's living like a queen over there." Dekeisha, Alexis

Duvall, Marcie Bee, and Lisa Snow were standing with The Fabulous Five by the school fence, and Jana had just finished reading Christie's letter aloud.

"Yeah," agreed Lisa. "Before you know it, she'll be on speaking terms with Princess Di."

"Well, you know our Christie," said Beth, grinning proudly. "*Everybody* likes her."

Melanie nodded enthusiastically.

"Are you guys still going to call yourselves The Fabulous Five now that Christie's gone?" asked Dekeisha.

"You make it sound as if she's dead," grumped Katie.

"I didn't mean it to sound like that," said Dekeisha defensively. "I just meant . . . you know . . . it'll probably be a long time before Christie comes back. I just thought, since there are only the four of you, you might not call yourselves that anymore."

Jana looked determined. "There's no reason for us to change anything. Christie just lives in another town. We can write her lots of letters and even talk to her on the telephone. It will be almost like she's here."

Alexis raised her eyebrows. "Do you know what long-distance phone calls to England cost?"

"It doesn't make any difference," said Beth. "We'll pool our allowances and baby-sitting money to pay for it."

"And we'll call in the evening, when the rates are cheaper," Melanie said, looking pleased that she had thought of the idea.

"In the evening? What about the time difference?"

asked Marcie. "Isn't there something like five hours between here and there?"

"Let's see," said Dekeisha, squinting her eyes as she made a mental calculation. "That means if you call her at eight in the evening, it will be one o'clock in the morning where Christie is."

"Whoops. I forgot about that," said Melanie. She looked deflated for a moment, then added brightly, "We'll call her on weekends!"

"I wish you luck," said Lisa.

"Me, too," said Marcie. "I think it's going to be tough for you guys to keep The Fabulous Five the way it always has been."

"We can do it," declared Jana firmly. She looked at the other members of The Fabulous Five for support.

"Right!" they said in unison.

CHAPTER

3

"Can we sit with you guys?" asked Heather Clark as she and Sara Sawyer came up to the cafeteria table where Jana, Katie, and Melanie were sitting.

"Sure," said Melanie. "Just leave room for Beth."

"Okay, but everybody spread out if you see Marcie Bee heading this way," said Sara. "She's driving me crazy, trying to get me to ask Derek Travelstead if he likes her."

"Have a seat," said Jana. "Did you know we got a letter from Christie?"

"Alexis told us," answered Heather. "Isn't it wild how Marcie's been chasing Derek? I keep telling her that he'll never like her if she doesn't cool it. But will she listen? Of course not."

"And now she's trying to get me to talk to him be-

17

cause I sit next to him in English class," continued Sara. "What a pain."

Katie frowned. Who cared if Marcie Bee was chasing Derek Travelstead? There were more important things to think about.

"Christie said that when her family went through customs, a lady agent checked their passports," said Katie. "That proves that women are doing all kinds of jobs that only men used to do, even in England."

Just then Beth brought her tray to the table. "Hi, Heather. Hi, Sara," she said, slipping into an empty seat. She turned to the rest of The Fabulous Five and went on, "Why don't we buy one of those 'we miss you' cards for Christie. We can get our boyfriends to sign it, too."

"That's a great idea," said Jana.

"What about Chase Collins?" Melanie asked, directing her question to the other members of The Fabulous Five. "Should we ask him if he'd like to sign it, too?"

"Look out," warned Heather, interrupting. "I see Marcie Bee, and she's looking around for someplace to sit."

"Quick, hide me," begged Sara, ducking behind Katie.

"I don't know about asking Chase," said Katie, frowning at Sara and then turning her attention back to the others. "She broke up with him because he lied to her about having a history test so she'd let him copy her homework."

"*And* he talked her into breaking curfew. That one got her grounded," Beth reminded them.

"I think she still likes him, though," said Melanie.

Suddenly Sara stood up and picked up her tray. "Well, *ex-CUSE* me!" she said angrily. "I guess Heather and I are just too *boring* to be included in your conversation."

"Oh, no," insisted Jana. "We want you to sit with us, don't we, guys?"

"Sure," said Katie, and Melanie and Beth nodded.

Heather and Sara exchanged looks, and then Sara sat down again.

"Okay," she said. "I guess I just misunderstood."

"Randy told me that Chase has straightened out since all that happened," Jana continued. "The guys made him realize what a jerk he was. I think he's really sorry now."

"Maybe we could put something in the letter you're writing Christie, too," offered Sara. "We could say hi and that we're thinking about her."

"I know she'd like to hear from everybody from Wacko Junior High," said Jana. "Why don't I give you her address, and you can write her yourself? It's really neat. She lives on Queen's Pudding Square."

"We'd like to send her things just from us," explained Katie. "You know . . . The Fabulous Five has always been kind of special."

Heather and Sara looked at each other.

"Yeah, sure," said Heather with an edge in her voice. "Well, give me the address sometime—when you're not too busy."

While Heather was talking, Sara looked around the

cafeteria. "There are some seats over by Laura McCall and her friends. I need to talk to them about something. I'll see you guys later."

Heather jumped up. "Me, too." She followed Sara.

"What's wrong with them?" asked Melanie.

"Beats me," said Beth.

"Why don't we stop by the drugstore after school and get a card for Christie," suggested Jana. "Then we can go to Bumpers and get the boys to sign it."

"Let me be the one to talk to Chase," volunteered Melanie. "I'll find out if he still likes Christie."

"Maybe someone else ought to talk to him," said Katie. "You'd come back with the story that he's slowly dying of love sickness and only has two months to live, when his real problem is indigestion from eating cafeteria food."

Melanie stuck her tongue out at Katie, and the others laughed.

"Why don't I have Randy ask Chase if he still likes Christie?" offered Jana. "They're pretty good friends. Chase will tell Randy the truth."

They all agreed.

"What are you looking for, Jana?" asked Funny Hawthorne, walking into the yearbook room between second and third periods. "Maybe I can help."

Jana smiled appreciatively. She liked Funny, even though Funny was a member of the rival clique, The Fantastic Foursome, which included Laura McCall,

Melissa McConnell, and Tammy Lucero. Jana and Funny had developed a real friendship working as seventh-grade coeditors for *The Wigwam*.

"I'm looking for a couple of pictures for Christie," said Jana as she thumbed through a stack of photos. "The ones of the Super Quiz and homework hot-line teams. She's in both, and I want to send her copies. I know they're around here somewhere."

"I think I know where they are," said Funny, pulling open a desk drawer. "Here, and here's a picture of Chase Collins accepting a swimming medal, in case you want to stick that in, too," she added with a grin. "Just ask me where something is, and I'll come up with it. I may look disorganized, but there is a system to my mess."

"Thanks." Jana returned the smile. She glanced down at the picture of Chase. Funny was right, she thought. Christie would really appreciate getting that.

"Jana . . . uh . . . I want you to know that, in case you hear jokes about The Fabulous Five going around, I didn't have anything to do with them."

"Jokes?"

"Yes. Like, 'The Fabulous Five may have lost only one of its members, but it lost half of its brains.'"

Jana's lips tightened. "Laura's making jokes about us?"

Funny shrugged. "I didn't say that." Then she grinned. "Let's just say that if she found out I told you this much, she'd kill me. Oh, well!" she said, tilting her head and throwing up her hands. "She's killed me before, so one more time won't hurt."

"Thanks," said Jana, laughing at Funny in spite of herself. "You're a good friend."

Jana gathered up her things and headed out the door to her next class.

"Hi, Jana."

She turned to look into Randy Kirwan's blue eyes. She and Randy had been going together since the sixth grade, and even before then they had been friends.

"Sorry if I startled you," he said.

"That's okay. I wanted to talk to you, anyway. We were wondering if Chase might want to sign a card we've got for Christie. Does he still like her?"

Randy shrugged. "I don't know for sure, but I can ask."

"Would you?"

"Sure, but it's not going to do either of them much good, is it? They may not see each other again, anyway."

Jana stiffened. "You don't know that for sure. Her father got transferred over there. He can get transferred back," she said defensively.

Randy looked at her sympathetically. "Hey, I know how much you girls miss Christie. Believe it or not, I miss her, too. So do the other guys." His voice softened. "Things just don't happen that way in real life, Jana."

"I know," she said, looking away so he couldn't see

the dampness in her eyes. "But right now it's easier for me to think that they might."

"I'll talk to Chase," he said, taking her hand and squeezing it.

"I'm here!" Beth called out as she opened the door to Jana's room. She was carrying a large sheet of poster-board and had a camera case slung over her shoulder. "You didn't eat all the goodies, did you?"

"Your soda's on the desk getting warm, and Melanie's got the chips. You'll have to fight her for them," said Katie.

"What's the posterboard for, Beth?" asked Melanie.

"I've got another super idea, which I'll tell you about as soon as you let me have some of those potato chips."

"It had better be good," warned Melanie, tossing the bag at her.

"While Beth's stuffing her face, did everyone bring their letter to Christie?" asked Jana.

Melanie waved a sheet of paper, Katie held up two pages, and Beth pointed to her purse.

"I've got a couple of pictures of her and one of Chase accepting his swimming medal to put in, too," said Jana.

"No one moaned too much about how badly we miss her, right?" asked Katie. "Remember, we don't want her to think we're feeling bad, or that it's all her fault."

The other three shook their heads.

"Okay, I've already addressed an envelope to Christie, so we can put our letters into it, said Jana."

Melanie and Katie handed theirs over.

"Don't seal it! Don't seal it!" said Beth, bouncing up from the bed, where she had taken a seat. Potato chips spilled onto the floor.

"Don't worry. We'll put yours in, too," Katie told her.

"That's not what I mean," said Beth. "It's my idea! I thought of a way we can show Christie she's still part of The Fabulous Five." She looked around to be sure she had everyone's attention.

"What we're going to do, see, is tape this posterboard to the wall, and use Magic Markers to draw a picture of Christie on it. Then we'll get Jana's mother to take a picture of us standing next to it with my parents' Polaroid camera so we can send it to Christie."

"Beth, for once, one of your goofy ideas makes sense," said Katie.

"I love it," exclaimed Melanie, jumping up. "What part of Christie do I get to draw?"

"I've got tape," said Jana, digging into her desk drawer.

The posterboard was on the wall in seconds, and The Fabulous Five were hard at work drawing.

Katie drew a circle for Christie's head, while the others worked on her body.

"A tennis outfit! She has to be wearing a tennis outfit," said Jana.

"Yeah," agreed Katie. "And she needs a racket in her hand."

"Her nose isn't turned up like that, Melanie," complained Jana.

"It's the only kind I can draw."

"Here, let me do the mouth," said Katie. "You'll make her look like E.T."

When they were finished, they stepped back and looked at their masterpiece.

Beth covered her mouth to stifle a giggle. "She looks kind of funny."

"But it's definitely Christie," said Katie. "*Definitely*."

"Do you think she'll recognize herself?" asked Melanie.

"If we write her name on her shirt," replied Jana, printing it quickly with a black marker.

"Get your mom so she can take our picture, Jana," said Beth.

The girls pretended to put their arms around the cartoon of Christie as Jana's mother took their picture. Mrs. Pinkerton was laughing so hard she could hardly hold the camera steady.

"There. That's it," said Jana, dropping the Polaroid shot into the envelope with their letters and the other pictures.

"I'll mail it for you tomorrow, if you'd like," offered Jana's mother. "It needs to go to the post office for the extra postage to England."

"Thanks, but we want to do it ourselves, Mom," said Jana. "It's awfully special."

"Right," chorused the others.

CHAPTER

4

Christie opened the envelope eagerly and took out the first letter. It was from Melanie.

Dear Christie:

Boy, do we envy you in England. Please send lots of postcards.

Things are great here, too. Marcie Bee is making an idiot out of herself chasing Derek Travelstead. Everyone in school is talking about it.

We all went to the movies last weekend and to Taco Plenty later. Shane said to say hi. He said Igor said to tell you hi, also. Sometimes I think he actually believes that iguana can talk!

Jana, Beth, Katie, and I went to the mall on Satur-day. We wandered around and talked to lots of kids, the

*way we always do. Everybody asked about you. We had
lots of fun.*

That's all I can think of to write. We miss you.
Love,
   Melanie

Christie read the rest of the letters. They had pretty
much the same news.

But the most exciting things in the envelope were
the pictures—including one her friends had taken beside a drawing they had made and taped to the wall,
and one of Chase.

"That's me!" Christie gasped when she looked at the
drawing in the picture. It looked so funny, she laughed
out loud. The picture was like something a little kid
would make, with stick arms and legs, and eyelashes
that looked like the spokes of a wheel. Then her laughter died away. The girls were making silly faces and
were obviously having a great time. Seeing them having so much fun gave her an empty feeling in the pit of
her stomach. Before, she had done everything with
them, but now . . .

Christie tried to shake off a feeling of resentment.
What did she expect them to do, go into mourning
because she was gone? No, that was silly. But couldn't
they have said they missed her a little more?

She was looking at the pictures of herself with the
Super Quiz and hot-line teams when her mother called
from downstairs. "Christie! It's time to leave."

Christie gritted her teeth as she tucked the letters

and pictures back into the envelope and put it in the top drawer of her desk. The moment she had been dreading had come. Today was her first day of school in London.

Her parents had enrolled her in St. Margaret's, a private school for girls. The previous Monday she and her mother had taken a bus there to get her class schedule. The lady at the registration desk had pronounced it "shed-jewel."

That was when Christie had learned, to her complete puzzlement, that private schools were called *public* schools in England. When she had asked if public schools were called private schools, the lady had answered with a sympathetic smile, "No, dearie. They're called *council* schools." That didn't make sense to Christie, either. She supposed that sooner or later, she would understand.

She had also learned that kids from five to eighteen years old went to St. Margaret's. If her family stayed in London she could be going there for *five whole years*. She had gulped and realized that she had better like St. Margaret's.

After she had her schedule, Christie and her mother had gone shopping for her uniform. It consisted of a blue skirt and a blue blazer with a gold St. Margaret's school crest on the pocket. She also got a blue sweater with a crest to wear some days in place of the blazer. This was topped off with a hat that Christie wouldn't have been caught dead wearing at home. The crown was round like a man's derby, and it had a wide, flat brim.

Christie picked up her books and stopped to look at herself in the full-length mirror. She positioned the hat several ways before giving up on making it look right. All I need is an umbrella, she thought, and I'll look like a teenage Mary Poppins.

Her mother was waiting by the front door. "Hurry or you'll miss your bus, Christie. If you need anything, sweetheart," she said, kissing Christie on the cheek, "I'll be right here. So don't hesitate to call." She seemed as nervous as Christie.

There were a number of boys and girls, as well as adults, at the bus stop when Christie got there. The boys wore slacks with matching sweaters or blazers with crests on the pockets, and the girls wore skirts with matching sweaters or blazers. Christie knew that the different color combinations indicated which school the kids went to, and that the blazer or sweater with a crest meant you were going to a public school. Boys and girls went to separate public schools in England.

A tall, red double-decker bus pulled up at the stop. Christie let the other kids get on first, trying not to notice how happily they were chattering with each other. Then she climbed aboard, put her money in the coin box, and went up the stairs to the upper deck, where she found an empty seat near the back.

As the bus lurched from stop to stop, Christie watched the school kids get on. At one stop, two girls with St. Margaret's uniforms took seats opposite her. They were about her age. She wondered if either of them would be in any of her classes.

One had light brown hair that was cut short in front and on top and long in back. She punched a boy in the seat in front of her on the shoulder and started talking to him. He had soft blond hair that swept across his forehead and very straight features. The girl's dramatic gestures and facial expressions reminded her of Beth.

The other girl had dark brown hair and a pleasant face. She reminded Christie of Jana. Christie half wished she would notice her and speak to her.

Finally the bus pulled up at the stop next to St. Margaret's. Christie hung back as long as she could, letting the other girls get off before she left her seat. The girl with the short hair waved good-bye to the boy as she got off.

Christie looked up as she stepped onto the sidewalk. St. Margaret's loomed in front of her. Its gray stone walls were three stories high. Tall parapets at the corners of its roof made it look like a miniature castle. A sign carved in stone next to the front door said the building had been constructed in 1740.

Christie sighed, remembering Wakeman Junior High, the neat, modern school she had left behind. This building was depressing in comparison.

Instead of the grass that surrounded Wakeman, the school yard was concrete and was bordered by a tall chain-link fence. Little girls in identical blue jumpers ran and played among older girls wearing blazers and skirts like Christie's. She was glad to see they were also wearing the silly-looking hats. She would have died if she had been the only person wearing one.

Taking a deep breath, Christie walked onto the school grounds. She moved slowly among the girls, trying to appear unconcerned and at home. Maybe people would think she was looking for a friend. To her relief, the school bell finally rang.

Christie went to the room where she had been told to go to register each morning. Back home they called it homeroom. When she got there, the other girls were talking in groups of twos and threes. She found a seat near the back of the room, where she hoped she could just disappear.

To her surprise, the girl who had been on the bus and reminded her of Jana was in the seat next to her. The girl looked at Christie and actually smiled.

Gradually the talking quieted as the teacher, a large, stern-looking woman, peered over her glasses at the class and made checks in a book. The woman at the registrar's office had told her the teacher's name was Miss Woolsey.

Miss Woolsey's eyes came to rest on Christie, and Christie felt like a butterfly that had just been pinned to a mat. "I believe you're Miss Winchell, are you not?"

Christie pushed down a feeling of panic. "Yes, ma'am."

"Would you stand, please, Miss Winchell?"

Everyone in the room was suddenly looking at Christie. She could feel her face turning red.

"Class, I want you all to look carefully. This is *Miss Christie Winchell.*" She spoke the name very slowly and concisely.

Christie wanted to sink into the floor.

"Miss Winchell is your new classmate. I want you all to welcome her properly."

There were dutiful murmurs of "Hello" and "Pleased to meet you" from the class. Christie had the feeling that this was one teacher for whom you did exactly as you were told.

"Miss Winchell is from the United States. You will, of course, make her at home and treat her as ladies *always* treat a guest." It had the definite ring of an order.

Christie was thankful when she was allowed to sink back into anonymity.

The rest of the morning went well enough, although except for quick smiles from a couple of girls, no one made any special effort to be friendly. Christie was relieved that she understood enough not to make some big goof. She was beginning to relax when lunchtime came, and she went to the cafeteria.

As she stood in line waiting her turn, she glanced around the room. It was nothing like the cafeteria at Wakeman. It was old and gloomy, like the rest of the building. A teacher was sitting at the head of each table.

"How awful," Christie murmured. "How can anyone carry on a private conversation with a teacher listening in?"

The tables appeared to be arranged in order of age, with the younger children sitting at the far wall and the older ones at the opposite end of the room.

Christie scanned the room again, looking for a familiar face. Sitting alone in class was one thing, but in the cafeteria it would be a disaster. Just then she saw the two girls who had been on her bus at one table. Other girls who had been in her morning class were at the same table, with Miss Woolsey at the head, so Christie guessed she was supposed to sit there, too.

But will anyone talk to me? she wondered, and a new sense of panic engulfed her. What if no one talks to me but Miss Woolsey?

Don't be silly, she told herself sternly. If nobody talks, just concentrate on your food. After all, you have to eat.

The line moved forward, and Christie peered over the shoulder of a younger girl in front of her to see what was being served. There were none of the things she was used to having for lunch, like hamburgers, lasagna, sloppy joes, or pizza slices. She wrinkled her nose. Instead the waiters were serving up a casserole that looked as if it was made of chunks of meat in gravy with some kind of baked topping. Beside it they were spooning carrots and green beans. The meal was more like dinner than lunch.

Christie accepted a plate of food, took a carton of milk and a bowl of pudding, and headed for the table.

"Is anyone sitting here?" she asked, trying her best

to sound friendly. Two girls moved their chairs and trays to make room for her.

"You're the new girl from the States, aren't you?" asked the girl across the table. Christie remembered her from history class. She was small and had red hair. She looked a lot like Katie Shannon.

"Yes, I am. I'm Christie Winchell."

"I'm Eleanore Geach."

"Hi," responded Christie, glad for the first friendly gesture of the day.

"And I'm Phoebe Mahoney," said the girl from the bus who resembled Jana.

"I'm Nicki McAfee," said the girl who reminded Christie of Beth. Other girls introduced themselves. Christie had trouble catching all their names.

"Hi," said Christie, trying to include everyone. She waited for a second, hoping one of them would say something else. When no one did, she went back to her food. She poked at it and wrinkled her nose as she tried to figure out what it was.

"Shepherd's pie," said Eleanore.

"What?" asked Christie.

"What's on your plate. It's shepherd's pie. It's beef and gravy with mashed potatoes on top. We have it lots."

"Oh." Christie heard a giggle from somewhere down the table.

Miss Woolsey frowned the giggler into silence.

"You remind me of one of my best friends back home," Christie told Eleanore.

"I do?"

"Yes. Her name's Katie Shannon, and you look a lot like her." She turned to Phoebe. "It's funny, but you look like one of my other very best friends, Jana Morgan. And you look like Beth Barry," she said to Nicki. "I've got another friend named Melanie Edwards back home. We call ourselves The Fabulous Five," she explained with pride.

"Sounds kind of airy-fairy to me," remarked Nicki. There was sarcasm in her voice. "It's for dead cert I'm not any Beth Barry or whatever her name is."

"Airy-fairy?" echoed Christie.

Phoebe frowned at Nicki. "Never mind her, Christie. She's just being ratty. Mind your manners, Nicki, or I'll snitch on you."

Nicki looked to see if Miss Woolsey was watching and made a face at Phoebe.

Christie decided not to say anything more about The Fabulous Five. If it meant the others were going to make fun of her, she didn't want any part of it. Instead she concentrated on eating the shepherd's pie. It was actually very good. The only problem was, she figured she'd gain about fifty pounds a week eating lunches like this every day.

Christie could hardly wait for lunch period to be over. Except for a few more words she and Eleanore exchanged and a few glances from Phoebe, Christie felt totally left out of the conversation at the table.

It was Nicki who dominated the table talk, and the more Christie watched her, the more she felt she *was* a lot like Beth. All Nicki needed was to have on a wild outfit instead of a uniform. Her hair was already almost as spiky as Beth's.

It was easy to see that Phoebe, Eleanore, and Nicki were best friends. Watching them only made Christie more homesick.

Gradually the crowd in the dining room thinned, and Christie found herself sitting alone. She bit down hard on her lower lip as she felt tears welling up in her eyes. Getting up slowly, she picked up her tray and took it to the return. Even the woman collecting the dirty dishes didn't look at her. For the first time in her life, Christie felt as if she didn't exist.

CHAPTER

5

"Guess what!" shouted Beth as she ran across the school yard, waving a letter. She came to a screeching halt in front of Melanie, Katie, and Jana. "Look, look! I've got a letter from Christie."

"Why didn't you call and read it to us last night?" asked Katie.

"My dumb brother Brian brought in the mail yesterday and didn't tell me I had a letter until this morning." She unfolded the letter as the others huddled together to see.

Dear Beth:

Oh, dear, what shall I do next? Should I visit the Tower of London, where all those people were beheaded, or should I go to Buckingham Palace and visit the queen? Such difficult decisions to make. Ha!

Hi, Beth! It's your turn to get a letter from the world traveler, Christie Winchell. I decided to write to each of you in turn, and to make it fair, I put your names on pieces of paper and drew them from a bag. Jana's was first, and yours was second. I'm not going to tell who's next. Let Katie and Melanie wonder.

I went to school for the first time today. It's called a public school, which is strange, since it's actually a private school. Its name is St. Margaret's. There are a lot of different things over here, like the double-decker bus I have to take to get to school. You look down at everyone on the sidewalks.

Everyone wears a uniform at St. Margaret's. Girls our age wear the blue skirts and blazers. I'm not too wild about the hat that goes with it, though. And you have to wear the same thing every day. Beth, you'd go crazy.

Guess what? I met some girls today. One of them reminded me of you, and two others remind me of Jana and Katie. I haven't found a Melanie yet, but tell her I'll keep looking. Maybe I'll start a new Fabulous Five over here, or at least another chapter.

Tell Melanie not to be too envious. She'd hate it at St. Margaret's. It's an all-girls school. Maybe that's why I haven't found anyone who reminds me of Melanie yet. I'm not worried, though. Where there are girls, there have to be boys.

I loved that picture you drew of me with you guys

standing next to it. And tell Jana thanks for the picture of Chase. Mom says the things we had shipped won't get here for a few weeks. All my picture albums are packed in those cartons, so I don't have much to look at and remember you by.

Say hi to everybody for me, and write soon.
Love,
Christie

"Gosh, it sounds as if she's having a ball," said Jana. "Leave it to Christie to fit right in with no sweat."

"Do you suppose she's actually going to get to see the queen?" asked Melanie.

"She was just teasing," said Katie. "That's a sure way to tell when things are going well for people. They joke a lot."

"I can't imagine her meeting someone like you, Beth," teased Jana. "I didn't think there could be two people like you in the world."

"Ditto, you," replied Beth, laughing. "Do you suppose the other Jana has a boyfriend who looks like Randy?"

"And the other Katie dates a macho man like Tony?" Jana responded.

"Well, I'm jealous because she hasn't met anyone like me," said Melanie, sticking out her lower lip.

"Wouldn't it be something if she did start another group called The Fabulous Five in London?" mused Katie.

"Think about it," said Beth. "Maybe she'll start Fabulous Five groups in France and Germany, too." Her eyes grew big. *"There could be Fabulous Five groups all over the world. It would be totally awesome."*

"I think it would be totally *awful*," said Jana. "I mean, The Fabulous Five is special."

"I know," said Melanie. "You don't think Christie really will replace us with new friends, do you?"

"Of course not," said Katie.

Beth's eyes glazed over, and the other girls' talking faded. *I wonder what she's really like, that girl Christie says is like me,* she thought. *Does Christie like her as much as she does me? She really couldn't, could she? She hasn't known her that long, and Christie and I have known each other for years and years. Still . . . Christie seems to think the girl is special. Hmmm.*

Jana bit back a feeling of disappointment. *Christie is making friends really fast,* she thought, *and I'm glad. But I hope she doesn't call them The Fabulous Five. We've always been special. Should I tell Christie how I feel?*

Someone just like me? thought Katie. *I have to admit, I never thought I'd hear that. It's funny. Christie always told me how different I am, but already she's found someone "just like me." I wouldn't tell her, but it hurts a little to know it was so easy.*

Melanie took in a deep breath to help hold back a sob. *I don't care how many new friends Christie finds in London.*

I still miss her a lot. She's one of us and always will be. I kind of wish she had said she had met someone like me, though. It would have meant she's thinking about me the way she is about the others. Melanie let out her breath and smiled at her friends. They all seemed awfully quiet.

Katie finally broke the spell. "I brought the 'missing you' card for all of us to sign and mail to Christie," she said, reaching into her purse and pulling out an envelope.

"Are we going to ask Chase to sign it?" asked Beth.

"I'll see Randy first period and find out if he asked Chase," answered Jana. "Then we can get the guys to sign it at Bumpers after school."

"Christie seemed to like the things we sent her," said Katie. "Maybe we should send her something else."

"Yeah," agreed Melanie. "Especially since she hasn't gotten all her things yet."

"Why don't we all go through our albums and send her pictures of us together?" suggested Beth. "That way she'll remember all the good times we've had."

"Great idea," said Jana. "And we can give them to you to put in your letter to Christie."

"What about calling Christie?" asked Beth. "When are we going to do that?"

"I think we ought to find out how much it costs first," said Katie. "Then we'll know how long we can talk to her. I'll ask mom to help me find out."

"Great," said Jana, and the four girls drifted off to their classes.

* * *

"Who hasn't signed Christie's card yet?" asked Katie. She, Jana, Beth, and Melanie were sitting in a booth in Bumpers, the fast-food restaurant where all the junior high kids hung out.

Melanie checked the names. "We've got everybody. I'm really glad Chase wanted to sign it."

"Me, too," said Jana. "It's funny how Christie and Chase had to actually break up for him to realize how much he likes her. Randy said Chase even wants Christie's address."

"Love triumphs over all!" said Melanie, blowing kisses into the air with both hands. "Now all we have to do is take this card to the post office and mail it."

"Look out," whispered Beth. "Here come Laura McCall and her friends."

Laura was headed for their booth, with Melissa, Tammy, and Funny right behind.

"Well, if it isn't The Fabulous Five minus one," said Laura. "I see you're still hanging out together."

"You wish we wouldn't, don't you, Laura McCall?" retorted Beth. "We'll be friends long after your group has split up."

"Oh, is that so?" said Laura, gloating. "Alexis Duvall said you let her read Christie's latest letter. I heard she's already found another group of friends to take your place, and she's going to call *them* The Fabulous Five. It didn't take her long to replace you guys, did it?"

Melissa and Tammy were smiling and nodding behind her. Funny looked as if she'd rather be someplace else.

"She has *not* replaced us!" Jana said emphatically. She was so angry that she slammed down her soda, and it splashed on her shirt. "What do you expect her to do, act unfriendly to everyone in her new school?" she asked dabbing at her blouse with a napkin.

"Of course not, but that's different from replacing such totally awesome friends," Laura scoffed. "And from what I heard, she's found someone to replace all of you except Melanie. I guess the rest of you were probably easy, but she'll have a hard time finding someone as boy crazy as you, Melanie."

Melanie looked as if she were going to explode. But before she could say anything, Laura twirled, whipping her long braid behind her shoulder.

The Fabulous Five stared after her. Their eyes were shooting fire.

"Christie's wanting to have friends just like us is a compliment," said Katie, sticking out her chin defiantly. "We're special to her. So why *wouldn't* she want to hang around other people like us?"

"That's right," agreed Beth. "That just proves how much we mean to her."

"Excuse me a minute," said Jana, getting up. "I've got to wash the soda off my hands."

Jana was drying her hands in the girls' room when the door opened and Funny Hawthorne came in.

"I'm sorry about what happened out there," said

Funny, grimacing. "Laura just can't help taking shots at you guys."

"It's not your fault, Funny. I know how you really feel, and so do the others. It just makes me mad that Laura's trying to break up our friendship with Christie just because Christie's moved."

Funny bit her lip and looked down at her shoes. When she looked up, she spoke softly. "Jana, can I tell you something without your getting mad?"

Jana stopped drying her hands and smiled at Funny. "Sure. You know you can."

"Some of the kids have been talking. I don't mean Laura, but kids like Alexis, Dekeisha, and Lisa. They say that all you guys in The Fabulous Five talk about anymore is how great Christie is." Funny paused before going on.

"Jana, it's almost as if Christie died, and you want to make sure you don't forget her. Everybody understands how much you miss her. She must miss you, too, but she said in her letter that she's starting to make friends. She's paying attention to the people around her over there." Funny looked pleadingly at Jana. "Have I said too much?"

Jana shook her head. Funny was a true friend. Jana was more sure of that than ever. It had taken a lot of courage for Funny to say what she just had. Jana stuffed her paper towel in the wastebasket and reached out, hugging Funny.

"No, you haven't said too much."

Jana remained in the girls' room after Funny left.

She needed to think. The conversation with Funny had jolted her. Was she right? Now that Jana thought about it, she remembered the strange expressions on some of the other kids' faces when The Fabulous Five talked about Christie. She, Katie, Melanie, and Beth were talking about a friend and the new things she was doing. But were they ignoring the people they were with every day?

When she went back to the booth, she asked, "Can you guys come over this evening after supper? We need to have a meeting of The Fabulous Five."

Melanie gave her a puzzled look. "You make it sound like an emergency."

"It is," Jana assured her.

CHAPTER

6

"*W*hat's up?" asked Katie as she walked into Jana's room that evening. Beth and Melanie were already there.

"We were waiting for you to start," Jana told her.

"Yeah," said Melanie, who was sitting on the bed with her feet tucked under her. "Were you waiting outside to make sure we were all here before you made your grand entrance?"

"No, silly." Katie plopped down on the bed next to her. "My mom and I were checking with the long-distance telephone operator on what it costs to call London. So there. I'll tell you about it after we hear what Jana has to say."

As Jana told the other girls about her conversation with Funny at Bumpers, their expressions turned serious.

"I don't think we've been talking about Christie too much," protested Beth vehemently. "What are we going to do, just forget that she exists?"

Katie frowned and shook her head. "No, of course not. But let's think about it a minute. Alexis and the others are our friends. They wouldn't have said what they did unless they really feel that way."

Melanie shrugged her shoulders. "Well, we can't just *quit* talking about Christie."

"Funny didn't say we should quit talking about her," responded Jana. "She just said we aren't paying attention to our other friends. They think we don't even hear what they're saying."

Katie pushed her red hair behind her ears. "Christie did say in her letter that she's meeting people and making new friends in London. It sounds to me as if she's adapting to being gone."

"Yes, it does," agreed Jana. "And I think that we need to get our lives back to normal, too. We need to be involved with people. We even need to decide if we want to stay just the four of us, or if we want to ask someone else to join The Fabulous Five. We haven't talked about that seriously yet."

Melanie's eyes grew big. "Someone else in The Fabulous Five?"

"There almost was once before," said Jana. "Remember in sixth grade when we asked Mona Vaughn if she wanted to be in our group?"

"Yes." Beth giggled. "And if she had said yes, we would have changed our name to The Sensational Six."

They all laughed at the memory.

"Christie says she met someone like Jana, Beth, and me at the school she goes to," reasoned Katie. "That means she's thinking about having friends like us there. There's no reason we can't find someone at Wakeman to fit into The Fabulous Five. It might make us feel better to have things more like they used to be."

"It might," said Beth.

"I agree," said Jana. "At least it's worth a try."

Melanie swung her feet down to the floor. "What about asking Alexis or Dekeisha? They're both really nice."

"Or there's Marcie or Sara," suggested Katie.

"Funny would be nice, too, if she didn't already belong to The Fantastic Foursome," offered Beth. "We know how much you like her, Jana."

"Yes, I do. But the person we pick should be *everyone's* favorite, not just mine. I think we should all vote, and it should be unanimous."

"Before we ask anyone, we need to see if she's right for The Fabulous Five. We should get her to hang out with us for a while," said Melanie. "Then we can see how she fits in."

"That's a good idea," said Katie. "But we can't let anyone know what we're doing. If Laura ever found out, she and her friends would laugh at us and make a big deal out of it in front of everyone."

Jana laughed. "I bet Laura's secretly *dying* to be in The Fabulous Five herself."

"Can you imagine if we asked *her* to join?" asked Beth, falling over backward on the floor and acting as if she were dead.

"I vote we try Alexis," said Melanie. "She's really nice, and we all like her."

"I second the motion." Beth sat up again. "She's a lot of fun."

"Tomorrow's Friday. Why don't we ask her if she'll go to the movies with us?" said Katie.

"And we can have a sleepover after that," suggested Melanie. "That way we can really get to know her."

"We can have it at my place," volunteered Jana. "Mom and Pink go bowling on Fridays, and we can have the apartment to ourselves."

"Now that we've got that decided, can we talk about what it costs to call London?" asked Katie. She had everyone's attention.

"The long-distance operator said if we call before one o'clock in the afternoon on a weekday, it will cost one dollar and forty-four cents for the first minute and ninety-four cents for each additional minute. If we call between one and six P.M., it's a dollar fifteen for the first minute and seventy-one cents a minute after that."

"Since there are four of us, we'll need to talk to Christie for at least half an hour when we call," said Jana. "How much would that cost?"

"Let me figure that out," offered Katie, scribbling

arithmetic on her paper. "It would be thirty dollars and fifty-three cents if we call in the morning, and twenty-four thirty-five if we called in the afternoon. That includes the taxes the operator told us about."

"Eeeyew!" cried Beth. "Don't we get a discount because we're under eighteen?"

Katie rolled her eyes in disbelief. "I can figure out what it would cost if we talked to her for only ten minutes."

"I don't want to hear it," Jana said firmly. "When there are just two of us on the phone, we talk for half an hour. If there are four of us talking to her, that's the absolute minimum."

"Gee, I'm broke," moaned Melanie.

"I'm close to it," said Beth.

"We can save up," said Jana. "It won't take us that long if we put our allowances together. Why don't we let Katie keep track of how much we have, and she can tell us when we've got enough?"

They all agreed.

"Wow!" exclaimed Melanie. "I need a soda. Making all these decisions has made me thirsty."

"Last one to the kitchen has to make the popcorn," called Jana, racing for the door.

"There's Alexis," whispered Beth. The Fabulous Five were at their favorite place by the school fence the next morning.

Alexis was standing under the gum tree with Sara

Sawyer and Heather Clark. The tree had a brightly colored trunk because kids stuck their bubble gum there as they entered the school.

"We can't talk to her while she's with Sara and Heather," whispered Katie. "We've got to get her alone."

"Well, we don't want Alexis to get suspicious about what we're doing, either," cautioned Jana. "We've got to act totally natural."

"I've got an idea," said Beth. "Melanie and I'll talk to Sara and Heather. We'll try to distract them and gradually move them away from Alexis. That way Katie and Jana can ask her if she'll go to the movies with us tonight."

"Good idea," said Melanie. "I'll take Sara. Beth, you take Heather."

The Fabulous Five put on their best smiles as they approached the three girls.

Sara saw them first and waved.

"I bet you've got another letter from Christie and want to show it to us," said Alexis. It was hard to tell if she was being sarcastic.

"No. We just came over to talk to you," replied Katie, grinning. "What's new?"

Melanie put her hand on Sara's shoulder and moved her away. "Sara, can I ask you a question about our history homework? I've really been having trouble with it, and I know you can help me."

"Maybe I can," said Sara, sounding flattered.

Beth tried the same tactic on Heather. "Oh,

Heather. I've been wanting to tell you about the neat idea I've got for some new earrings I'm making. You remember the ones I made out of fishing line, don't you?"

Heather nodded but refused to budge. "I remember."

Jana and Katie glanced at each other. No way could they ask Alexis to go to the movies with Heather so close.

"Uh, did you have fun at the all-school dance?" asked Jana.

Alexis got a puzzled look on her face. "Yes. But that was a couple of weeks ago. We talked about it, remember?"

"Oh, yeah," said Jana, looking at Katie for help.

"We just thought you might have forgotten to tell us something about your date with Bill Soliday," said Katie. "Did you two have fun?"

"Yes. We talked about that, too."

"Hi, everybody," called Lisa Snow as she and Marcie Bee came walking up. "What are you doing?"

"Nothing," answered Katie.

"We were just talking," said Alexis. "Hey, that's a neat sweater you've got on, Lisa. Is it new?"

The Fabulous Five looked at each other in frustration. There was no way they were going to get Alexis alone at that moment.

When the bell finally rang for school to start, The Fabulous Five hung back and went into the building together.

As they went through the door, Beth whispered, "Let's put a bounty on Alexis. Whoever gets her to go with us to the movies tonight, gets her lunch paid for by the others."

"It's a deal," Katie whispered back.

"We'll check in with each other at lunch," said Jana.

"Talk about tough," said Melanie. She looked exasperated when she joined The Fabulous Five in the cafeteria. "I thought I had Alexis cornered between first and second periods, and then Laura McCall butted in and started talking to her. The bell rang, and they went off together."

"I saw her in the hall twice, but before I could catch up with her, she went into a classroom," reported Katie. "Didn't *anyone* get Alexis alone?"

"I looked all over for her and was almost late for all my morning classes," said Jana.

The three of them looked at Beth. The corners of her mouth twitched, and then she got a big grin on her face. "My lunch costs two dollars and seventy-five cents," she announced. "You guys can pay me any time between now and the end of lunch period. I'll take it in small bills."

"All right, Barry! Can she go?" asked Jana.

"Yup. She'll meet us in front of Cinema Six. She even said she could go with us to Taco Plenty later."

"Now we can tell Christie not to worry about us,"

said Melanie. "She'll be happy that we're finding someone new to hang out with, just as she is."

"Right," said Jana. "I bet she's been worried about us."

"That's the kind of good-hearted person she is," remarked Katie.

CHAPTER

7

"*W*here's Alexis?" asked Katie as she joined Melanie, Beth, and Jana in front of Cinema Six.

"She's over there, talking to Sara and Heather," said Beth.

"Is she going to sleep over?" asked Melanie.

"Her things are already at my apartment," answered Jana.

"We'd better go in if we're going to get seats together," said Beth. "I'll go tell Alexis."

Beth was back shortly. "She said to save her a seat. She wants to see Marcie about something."

"There are five together," said Katie as they filed down the aisle.

"And they're right behind the guys," remarked Jana.

"And Chase is with them," added Melanie.

59

When they were seated, popcorn flew out of the row in front of them and landed all over the girls.

"Okay, wise guys," said Katie, pounding playfully on Tony Calcaterra's back. "You know littering is an offense punishable by twenty years in jail."

"We'll plead not guilty due to insanity," said Keith, tossing a kernel at her.

"You'd win easily," Jana told him, laughing. "You could get tons of people to testify that you're crazy."

"Especially us," said Beth.

Just then the theater lights dimmed, and Alexis worked her way into the row.

"Thanks for saving me a seat, guys," she whispered.

"Gee, that was a great love story," said Beth as the girls made their way out of the theater after the movie.

"I hate sad movies," commented Alexis. "I always get weepy, and then I look terrible. Are my eyes and nose all red?"

"No," said Jana. "I have the same problem, only I always look like Rudolph the Red-nosed Reindeer after I've been crying."

"Are we still going to Taco Plenty?" asked Melanie. "Love stories make *me* hungry."

"Oh, there're Lisa and Melinda," said Alexis. "I've got to talk to them. I'll see you guys at Jana's, okay?" She abruptly cut through a row to the other side of the theater.

The Fabulous Five stared after her.

"Maybe we should forget Taco Plenty and order out for pizza when we get to my apartment," said Jana. "I'd hate for Alexis to get there and not find us there."

Melanie shrugged. "Sounds like a good idea."

The Fabulous Five continued their discussion of Alexis in Jana's bedroom as they unrolled their sleeping bags.

"I don't feel like I saw her much tonight," said Beth. "The only time she was with us was when we were watching the movie."

"Hey, give her a break," replied Jana. "This is the first time we've hung out together."

"It was more like hanging out separately," commented Melanie.

Katie plumped up her pillow and settled back against it. "I agree with Jana. We won't be able to tell if Alexis fits in after just one try. Remember how long we knew each other before we realized we were best friends?"

Just then the doorbell rang.

"It's probably Alexis," said Jana as she dashed out of the room.

"I'll be the official caller," volunteered Melanie. "What kind of pizza does everyone want?"

"Sausage, as usual, for me," said Katie, leaning back against her pillow and stretching out her legs.

"Pepperoni and sausage for me," said Beth.

"Deep-dish, pepperoni, green pepper, and mushroom for me," said Jana, walking into the room with Alexis behind her.

"Hey! This is great," exclaimed Alexis. "I'm glad you guys invited me over. I'll have pepperoni on my pizza."

"Sounds good," said Jana. "You guys place the order, and Beth and I'll get the sodas."

Before long the pizza had been delivered and the floor was littered with boxes, paper plates, and napkins.

"Fabulous." Beth rubbed her stomach and licked her lips. "Why does pizza always make me feel as if I've died and gone to heaven?"

"Probably because you ate so much, you're going to blow up and go there," answered Katie.

"I didn't eat as much as you did, Katie Shannon. Count the crusts. You've got seven, and I've only got six."

"Oh, no you don't." Katie laughed. "I saw you eat two crusts."

"Instead of arguing about how much we ate, why don't we do something else?" asked Melanie.

"I agree," said Alexis. "I don't really care how many slices of pizza Beth and Katie ate."

"*Riingg!*" The phone rang, and Jana nodded for Melanie, who was closest, to take the call.

"Hello," said Melanie. She listened, and her face lit up.

She put her hand over the mouthpiece. "It's Chase!" she whispered.

She returned to the phone. "I told you we sent the card," she said with a grin.

"Has she said anything else about you in her letters?" Rolling her eyes, she repeated the other end of the conversation so they would know what was going on. "Maybe . . ."

Jana shook her head at Melanie. "You'd better not tell him," she mouthed.

Melanie nodded her head that she understood.

"I can't tell you *everything* we girls talk about, Chase," she teased. "Why don't you write Christie yourself and ask her? Her address? Just a minute."

Melanie hugged the phone to her chest so he couldn't hear. "*He's going to write Christie!* Quick, give me Christie's address."

Jana dug through a desk drawer and found Christie's letter.

"Do you have a pencil and paper?" Melanie asked. "Okay. It's Twenty Queen's Pudding Square."

As Melanie finished giving Chase the address, Alexis spread out her sleeping bag.

When Melanie hung up, she jumped out of her chair and spread her arms dramatically. "He's going to write her. Maybe their great romance isn't over yet."

"How far is London?" asked Katie. "Five thousand miles or so? I would say there's not much chance for a meaningful romance at that distance."

"Katie Shannon, you're too practical. I like to think that in love, where there's a will, there's a way."

"Christie hasn't mentioned any boys," said Jana. "I wonder if she has met any."

"Christie will have boys beating down her door," said Beth.

"Yeah, but she's going to an all-girls school," said Melanie, sticking out her tongue. "How's she going to meet boys?"

"Do you suppose they've got places like Bumpers where kids hang out after school?" asked Katie.

"They must," said Melanie. "It would be cruel and inexcusable punishment if they didn't have places where boys and girls can meet."

"Unusual punishment," corrected Katie.

"That, too," responded Melanie.

They talked about Christie a while longer before the sound of light snoring got their attention. The Fabulous Five turned in unison to look at Alexis. She had gone to sleep, hugging her pillow.

CHAPTER

Dear Christie:

Thanks for the letter. I was glad that you picked me to write to next. Melanie is about to die because you didn't write to her instead. She knows that you'll write to her soon, so it's okay.

I wanted to be the first one to tell you! If you haven't gotten it yet, you're going to be getting a card from us and the boys. And guess who signed it besides Keith, Shane, Randy, and Tony. Chase Collins! We had Randy ask Chase if he still likes you, and he said yes. We think he feels so bad about what happened between you and him that he has reformed. He asked us for your address, and we gave it to him.

And guess what else. Jana, Katie, Melanie, and I had a meeting of The Fabulous Five, only it wasn't really

The Fabulous Five without you. We decided to ask Alexis Duvall if she'd like to hang out with us. Five friends seems like a better number than four, and besides, we don't want anyone to mistake us for Laura McCall and The Fantastic Foursome. Ha!

Alexis has been sitting with us sometimes at Bumpers, and she went to the movies with us last night. Later we had a sleepover at Jana's house. The evening didn't work out too well, though. Alexis spent most of the time with other kids, then she fell asleep while we were talking.

Well, I'd better close for now. Write Melanie or Katie real soon and tell us more about what's happening out there in the big, wide world. Miss you lots.
Love,
* Beth*
P.S.: Since you don't have all your things from here yet, we're sending you some more pictures to remind you of us.

Christie's heart sank as she reread the part in Beth's letter about their asking Alexis to hang out with them. It sounded as if the others were doing very well without her. She hadn't *dreamed* they'd find someone to replace her in The Fabulous Five so quickly. Had it been that easy? Here Christie was in a new place without any friends, and her old friends were acting as if she never existed. Alexis is nice, but *I* wouldn't have picked her, she thought resentfully.

She reread the part about Chase Collins next. A lot

of good it did her to know he still liked her. She undoubtedly would never see him again.

The pictures brought a smile to Christie's face. There was one of them all at the animal shelter holding pets they had rescued from being put to sleep at Christmas. There was a picture of them on stage after Trevor Morgan, the leader of the rock band Brain Damage, asked them to come up. That was the time that Beth had gotten in trouble over bragging so much. There was a picture of The Fabulous Five at Adventureland Amusement Park with their boyfriends, when Wacko Junior High had the great TV turnoff. There was a picture of all of them at Bumpers, and even one of just the girls from the time they had the weird sleepover, when each had dreamed that she was one of the other Fabulous Five members.

Christie sighed. The pictures brought back all kinds of memories. Getting up, she went to the closet to get a small box she had been saving. She took all the letters and pictures from home and put them inside. This will be my magic box, Christie told herself. Whenever I feel lonely and blue, I'll get it out, and just like magic I'll feel better.

For right now, though, it made her realize how miserable her life had become. Her friends at home were looking for someone to take her place, and the boy she liked had decided *after* Christie had moved that he liked her. On top of that she hadn't made any friends at St. Margaret's. The one group of girls that looked as if they might be friends were already a clique, and Christie didn't know if they'd let her be part of their group. What more could possibly go wrong?

"How are things at the office, Vince?" Christie's mother asked that night at the dinner table.

"Great," he said exuberantly. "We're really getting things whipped into shape. Being here in London instead of commuting from the U.S. makes a big difference. Before you know it, I'll have this company fully integrated and running the way it's supposed to. How was your day?"

Christie's mother smiled at her husband. "I have to admit that things are going better for me than I ever thought they would. My new job at the University of London is very interesting. It's giving me all kinds of ideas about new career opportunities."

Christie picked at the food on her plate and thought gloomily about her own predicament as her parents talked.

"What about you, Christie?" her father asked.

"What?"

"How's it going in school? Are you meeting lots of nice kids?"

"Yes."

Silence followed.

"What are some of your new friends' names?" he asked.

Both of her parents were waiting for her to answer.

Should she tell them the truth and say she didn't have any friends at school? She felt as if she didn't have friends anywhere.

"Oh, there's Eleanore, and Phoebe, and Nicki," she fibbed.

Her father beamed at her. "That's pretty good for the short time you've been at St. Margaret's."

"Do any of your friends live nearby?" her mother asked.

Christie shrugged. "Don't know."

"Well, I'm sure the house will be full of teenagers before we know it," said her father. "It'll be just like old times with Beth, Melanie, Jana, and Katie coming by on Saturdays to congregate in your room or go to the mall."

"There aren't any malls in London, Vince," said Mrs. Winchell with a grin.

"Come to think of it, you're right," he responded cheerily. "Where do the kids from your school hang out, Christie?"

Christie shrugged again. "I don't know."

"Well, I'm sure you'll find out, dear. Kids have a way of finding each other, her mother said."

Her mother and father went back to their conversation.

Later, as Christie was finishing her homework in her room, she heard a light tapping on her door.

"Can I come in?" asked her mother, peeking in the door.

"Sure."

"How's the homework coming?"

"Okay," mumbled Christie.

"Christie, you don't seem very happy. Is everything really all right?"

Christie hesitated. She couldn't tell her mother how awful she felt. "Everything's fine."

Little frown lines appeared between her mother's eyes. "These girls, Eleanore, Phoebe, and what's her name . . . ?"

"Nicki."

"Yes, Nicki. Have you thought about having them over sometime?"

"No."

"Well, I think you should. Your father is right. It's about time we had some other young people in this house. Why don't you ask them here for a sleepover on Saturday? In fact, if you have other friends, you could invite them, too. Wouldn't that be fun?"

"What if they won't come?" asked Christie.

Her mother frowned. "Sure they will. Why wouldn't they?"

Christie shrugged again. "I don't know. Maybe they've got something planned already."

"Well, nothing ventured, nothing gained," Mrs. Winchell said, putting her arm around her daughter. "You invite as many girls as you want, sweetheart. Just let me know in time to have enough food. In fact if you want, we can bake cookies and really do it up right for your first housewarming. Everything will be fine," she said firmly. "You'll see." She patted Christie's hand and left.

Christie sagged in her chair. She knew that when her mother got that school principal sound in her voice and was even willing to cook, she was serious. There would be no changing her mind. Christie would have to have a sleepover.

She clenched her fists as she thought about having to ask Eleanore and Phoebe to a sleepover. Would they refuse? Worse yet, Christie wondered if she could even bring herself to ask Nicki, who hadn't been exactly friendly. If none of the three accepted, Christie would have to tell her parents that she really didn't have any friends in London. That would certainly shock them.

She pulled out her magic box and took out Beth's letter. She reread the part where Beth said she missed Christie. There was no way Beth could know how much Christie missed her and the rest of The Fabulous Five at that moment. In the past, when one of The Fabulous Five had problems, the others helped out. But Christie was all alone now, and no one could help her.

CHAPTER

9

"Darn!" said Christie as she grabbed at her hat to keep it from being blown away. Its wide brim made it into a perfect kite. Why did St. Margaret's make them wear such a stupid thing, anyway? It was only good for getting in the way.

Christie glanced around as she walked onto the school grounds. Phoebe, Eleanore, and Nicki were at their usual place in the corner, where the steps joined the school wall. It was almost as if they had chosen the spot to give themselves privacy from the other kids. Christie had felt like an intruder the few times she had gone over to them.

The girls were friendly enough, but the talk always changed to things Christie was unfamiliar with. At least half the time Nicki wanted to talk about a boy named Connie Farrell. Christie figured out he was the blond-haired boy on their bus, and Nicki had dated him a few times. Christie usually felt like a fifth wheel standing there listening to the girls' conversations and wandered off after a while.

Christie tried to decide what to do. Should she march over to the three girls and ask them to come to her sleepover? They did seem to be awfully engrossed in their conversation, and maybe they wouldn't like being interrupted. She decided not to disturb them right then. There would be a better time.

The wind lifted Christie's hat again, and she grabbed it, pressing her lips together tightly. Why was *she* the only one who seemed to be having trouble with the darn thing?

Rather than stand like a statue near the gate, making it plain for everyone to see that she didn't have any friends to talk to, Christie started casually wandering around the yard. Two girls she knew from her math class, Leslie and Rebecca, smiled at her but didn't call out to her to join them.

There were five girls talking and laughing near the fence. They looked like they were having a great time. Christie wondered if they were best friends and if they had a name for their group. Something like The Fabulous Five.

Feeling depressed, she decided not to wait for the bell to go into the school. She could at least put her hat in her locker and go over her homework. Anything would be better than standing around feeling invisible.

When she walked into the room, Miss Woolsey was at her desk, going over papers. The gray-haired teacher peered at Christie over the top of her glasses.

"Good morning, Miss Winchell," she said gruffly.

"Good morning, Miss Woolsey."

Miss Woolsey looked at her watch and back at Christie for a moment before returning to her work.

Christie opened a book and tried to look busy. Every few minutes the teacher looked her way. Was there a rule against coming in before morning bell? wondered Christie. Or did having kids in the room when she was doing her reports disturb Miss Woolsey? Christie tried to disappear behind her book.

When the bell rang, she watched the girls file into the room. They were chattering and laughing and having a good time, the way she used to at Wakeman Junior High.

"So how do you like it at St. Meg's?"

Christie whirled to find Phoebe standing next to her desk.

"St. Meg's?"

"It's what we call St. Margaret's."

"Oh, I like it," Christie responded. There was no way she could tell Phoebe how she really felt.

"Fitting in, are you? That's good. If there's anything I can help you with, let me know," the girl said cheerily as she headed for her seat.

"I will."

*   *   *

Later Christie saw Phoebe and Nicki walking in the hall together between second and third periods. Nicki was talking, and Phoebe was laughing. A twinge of envy went through Christie as they passed by without noticing her. They reminded her of how she had walked the halls of Wakeman zillions of times with her own friends. Christie decided to talk to Phoebe, Nicki, and Eleanore separately about the sleepover. It would be easier than facing them all at once and getting a mass rejection.

The rest of the day went quickly. She was learning that there were many differences between St. Meg's and Wacko Junior High, and they weren't just the uniform or the fact that St. Meg's was an all-girls school. While kids seemed to have fun at St. Margaret's, they didn't cut up the way Christie's classmates did at Wakeman. The teachers were always there to see that they kept to their business. Clarence Marshall from back home would last about one day with Miss Woolsey as his teacher, Christie thought.

The person in charge of the school was called a headmistress, instead of a principal. The headmistress at St. Margaret's was named Mrs. Tillington, and the kids all treated her like the queen of England.

Since Christie would eventually go to college, she was expected to take subjects right away that would prepare her for it. There would also be meetings between her parents and teachers about how well she was doing. Everything about the school said you should be trying hard to make good grades. That was the one thing Christie didn't mind. She had always been at the top of her class, and now she was regaining her confidence. It gave her one thing to feel good about.

She had also figured out what the kids did outside of school. There didn't seem to be an after-school hangout like Bumpers, the fast-food restaurant back home. Kids here mainly went to the films, or cinema—which was what they called the movies—or hung out at each other's homes.

Christie didn't know where to begin trying to fit in. For now she decided not to push it. Things would work themselves out . . . somehow.

Before she realized it, three-thirty had come and school was let out, and she hadn't had the opportunity to talk to Phoebe, Nicki, and Eleanore about sleeping over. Oh, well, she thought as she boarded the bus for home, I've got lots of time.

On Friday Christie still hadn't talked to the girls about Saturday night. Her mother had asked her about it a couple of times, and Christie had made excuses.

It was true, she had seen all three in the halls and in class. She had even talked to Phoebe and Eleanore once or twice, and Nicki had stopped to say something to her.

Whenever Christie talked to Nicki, she was left wondering whether Nicki was just naturally sarcastic or whether she didn't like Christie. She didn't know why Nicki wouldn't like her, but the girl's sharp manner was a little unsettling. Christie decided that Nicki was not like Beth after all, and would take a lot of getting used to.

That afternoon, between fourth and fifth periods, Christie saw Phoebe alone. She bit her lip and gathered her courage. If she was ever going to ask, she had better do it now.

"Hi," she said, falling in step beside Phoebe.

"Oh, hello."

"Phoebe, I was wondering . . ."

"Yes?" Pheobe looked at her quizzically.

"I was wondering if you might like to come to my house tomorrow evening and sleep over. We could watch TV and make popcorn," she added hurriedly. "I'm thinking about asking Eleanore and Nicki, too."

"Oh, that's a shame, Christie." Phoebe looked sincerely sorry. "If you had only asked me yesterday, I would have said yes. I've got something planned now."

"Oh, . . . that's all right," said Christie, smiling. "I meant to ask you sooner, but I just never seemed to have the chance."

"Another time then?" asked Phoebe. "We do have to get together. I think you're an all right person."

When they parted, Christie let out a sigh of relief. She had asked; that was the important thing. And the remark about her being an all right person was kind of nice.

Christie headed for her locker to exchange books. Since Phoebe couldn't go, should she still ask Eleanore and Nicki? What if Nicki could come, but Eleanore couldn't? Ooh, Christie thought. I'm not sure I'm ready to spend all that time alone with Nicki. Even if Eleanore was there, she was so quiet, it would be almost like being alone with Nicki.

While she was getting her books out of her locker, Christie made a decision. Now that she could truthfully tell her mother that she had asked someone, she would forget about the sleepover. She would try again when she knew Phoebe could come. Christie felt a lot better and hurried off to catch her bus.

CHAPTER

10

Dear Melanie:

Well, you win. You're the next one to receive a letter from me. Actually, I flipped a coin to see whether I'd write to you or Katie.

Things are fine here. My mother is working at the University of London, and she likes her job very much. My dad likes his, too.

One thing I forgot to mention in my other letters is my homeroom teacher, Miss Woolsey. She reminds me of our homeroom teacher at Mark Twain Elementary, Miss Wiggins. Remember how tough she was? Well, Miss Woolsey is ten times as tough. She looks over her glasses with little beady eyes that drill holes right through you. Nobody, I mean nobody, crosses her. The kids call her Old Laser Eyes.

I got the card and the pictures from you. The card was cute. I especially like that Chase wrote that he misses me. Why couldn't I have met him sooner? I'd like to write to him, but I don't know if I should. What do you think?

The pictures were super. Keep the cards and letters coming, okay?

Guess what. I almost had my first sleepover Saturday. Well, I was going to have one, but Phoebe, the girl who reminds me of Jana and whom I most wanted to come, couldn't, so I didn't ask the others. Next time I'll invite them earlier.

My parents and I went to the Tower of London on Sunday. Wow! What a place. It's like a walled fort and actually has lots of big towers. The guides told us about all the people who were imprisoned and killed there. Some had their heads cut off, some were hanged, and others were murdered in all sorts of gruesome ways.

There were even two little boys executed there. One was a twelve-year-old named King Edward V, and the other was his nine-year-old brother, Richard, Duke of York. They were imprisoned in the Bloody Tower. The guides say that sometimes visitors to the tower see the ghosts of two boys walking hand in hand, wearing white nightgowns. Isn't that wild?

We also got to see the queen's jewelry. There are gorgeous crowns, with diamonds as big as tennis balls, and jeweled scepters. Just all kinds of beautiful things. And, no, I didn't get any for you.

I need to close for now, Mel, and study. Tell everyone hi for me.
Love,
   Christie.

"Isn't that something about Christie's almost having a sleepover," said Jana. "I guess she really is making lots of friends."

The Fabulous Five were gathered in Melanie's family room. Katie was idly patting Rainbow, who was curled up on the couch at Katie's feet.

"Yeah," said Melanie. "And she's doing a lot of sightseeing."

Then Jana asked the question that had been nagging at her recently. "What do you think about Alexis?"

"What do you mean?" asked Beth.

"I mean, I'm not sure she's the right person for The Fabulous Five. She likes us fine, but she likes everyone else fine, too. When she went with us to Taco Plenty the other night, it was the same as when she went to the movie with us. She's hardly with us."

"Yeah," said Melanie. "It's been bothering me, too. That's one reason I called this meeting of The Fabulous Five."

"I'm sure she likes us," said Katie. "She always agrees to do things with us when we ask."

"Yeah," said Melanie. "But she's always running off to talk to somebody else. That's not criticism, it's just a fact. Alexis doesn't feel the same way about The Fabulous Five that Christie did."

"Does," corrected Beth.

"Okay, does." Melanie nodded. "I don't think Alexis wants to be pinned down to one group."

"I agree," said Katie. "It's too bad, because she's really nice. But I guess we have to face it. Alexis probably doesn't want to be a regular member of any group. She's having too much fun with everybody."

"Why don't we go to plan B and check Dekeisha out?" suggested Beth. "She was in the PEAK program with Christie. If she's in PEAK, she's smart, like Christie. And she's always talking to us."

Katie chuckled. "She'll probably have a book with her all the time, like Christie did. I even miss that about Christie."

"I was thinking," said Jana. "Maybe one of our problems with Alexis is we haven't shown enough interest in her. If we want to do better with Dekeisha, we ought to concentrate on talking to her about things that interest her."

"Like what?" asked Beth.

"Like acting," suggested Katie. "Dekeisha was one of the witches in the Wakeman Halloween skit with you and Laura McCall, Beth."

"You're right," agreed Melanie. "And she did the Bill Cosby monologue at the TV turnoff assembly. You love acting too, Beth, so you could talk to her about that."

"Katie," Jana added, "you're the smartest one of us

after Christie. You should have conversations with De-keisha about things that take brains to understand."

Katie wrinkled her nose. "Brainy conversations? What do you want me to say—'Hey, Dekeisha, let's talk about world affairs'? I don't think I'm in De-keisha's class."

"Sure you are, silly," said Jana. "You can find out what interests her the most and talk to her about those things."

Katie frowned as she thought that over.

"She goes with Don Petry, so she likes boys," said Melanie. "I could talk to her about my seven flirting tips."

"I'm not sure that would impress her," replied Beth. "But go ahead. If we work at it, we can be interesting enough for her to want to join The Fabulous Five. At least it's a plan."

Jana looked at Katie. "Now, how much more money do we need for our long-distance call to Christie?"

"I figured it out in math class today," answered Katie. "We need twenty-five dollars and ninety-seven cents for a half hour call. That's if we call her on a Saturday morning. If we call her in the afternoon, we need fourteen dollars and seventy-nine cents."

"Yikes! That's a lot," said Beth, making a face.

"I've got some change I can put in," offered Jana, digging in her purse.

"Me, too," chimed in Melanie.

The others went through their purses and contrib-uted, too.

"Now we need seventeen dollars and twenty-nine cents to call in the morning, or eleven dollars and eleven cents to call in the afternoon," announced Katie. "If we put in part of our allowances, it won't take too much longer."

"Not bad," said Melanie. "Now if somebody will help me, I'll get soda and cookies so we can celebrate the new Fabulous Five, and the upcoming phone call."

"I'll help," volunteered Katie.

"Me, too," said Jana and Beth.

"I'm going to write Christie back right away," said Melanie, as the four of them marched to the kitchen. "Does anyone have a picture or anything else to send or tell her?"

CHAPTER

11

Christie held the letter from Chase as if it might crumble in her hands. It had been in that day's mail, along with another from Melanie, when she got home from school. She had a fluttery feeling as she slowly read his words.

Hi, Chris:

I bet you're surprised to hear from me. I got your address from Melanie. The Fabulous Five tell me you write to them lots.

Wakeman's swim team is doing great. We won our last two meets, and I took several medals, which I'm not going to talk about, because you'll think I'm bragging, and I don't want you to think about me that way any-

*more. I know it was one of the things I used to do that
got me in trouble when you and I were dating.*

*The thing I want you to know is I haven't missed one
swim practice and haven't broken my curfew once since
you left. My mom and dad don't know what to think.
They keep asking me questions as if they're worried I've
committed a crime, and I'm trying to cover it up.
They're funny.*

*I keep thinking it's too bad that you had to leave before
I got myself straightened out. Maybe we would still be
dating.*

*From what The Fabulous Five tell me, you must be
pretty busy. If you ever get a chance in your busy schedule, I'd like to hear from you.*
Chase

Christie looked closely at the spot below his name.
Had he written in some X's and then erased them? A
feeling of frustration welled up in her. She knew all the
reasons her family had moved: It was a big promotion
for her father, and her parents hoped that living in
London would be good for all of them. But when the
boy she cared about told her he cared about her, too,
and he was miles and miles away, knowing those reasons didn't help.

Christie folded Chase's letter and put it back in its
envelope. Then she took out her magic box and sorted
through its contents until she found the picture that
Jana had sent of Chase accepting the swimming medal.

Next she pulled out a piece of ruled notebook paper

she had put in the box. On it Chase had written "C.C. + C.W." one night when they were doing homework together. At the bottom of the box, underneath the letters and pictures from her friends, she found a menu from Taco Plenty that she and Chase had used to draw pictures of each other on. She was glad that she had kept the paper and menu in her backpack instead of putting them with the things that were shipped separately.

She found a paper clip and fastened together all the things she had that reminded her of Chase. Then she put them in the very bottom of the magic box so she would know where they were when she needed to look at them.

Christie glanced out her window into the courtyard, where the shadows were darkening the corners of the buildings and doorways. The sky had been overcast ever since they had arrived in England. The drabness of the weather hadn't helped her mood. Didn't the sun ever shine?

Below, the old lady was puttering in her garden. Her cat was lying on the top step watching her every movement, its tail twitching nervously. The lady wore the same raincoat and scarf as always.

She reminded Christie of Grandma Winchell, who lived alone in Seneca Falls, New York. But Christie's grandma had a huge yard and mounds of flowers all around her big old house. The Winchells had gone there every Thanksgiving and Christmas. Christie could almost smell the wonderful aromas of those holidays at that very moment.

Going over to her bed, Christie hugged her tennis bear to her. It had been a present from her grandma.

Christie went back to her desk and picked up Melanie's letter. There were several pictures in it. Christie put them aside until she finished reading the letter.

Melanie said The Fabulous Five had been doing things with Alexis, but it wasn't working out. Melanie said she had begun to suspect it wouldn't when Alexis went to sleep early at a sleepover at Jana's while everybody was talking. Now they were thinking about asking Dekeisha to go places with them.

Christie looked at her bear. "Why do they have to replace me, anyway? What if Daddy gets transferred back home and there's already someone else in The Fabulous Five? Will they make room for me?" She couldn't imagine that they wouldn't, but she had to wonder.

"We were talking about you the other day," wrote Melanie, *"and Katie said she thought your favorite color was blue. Beth said no, it was pink. Then we started trying to remember who your favorite rock stars are, what your favorite album is, who your favorite actors are, all kinds of things. Everybody said something different, and we realized that we didn't know the answers. We've made a list of things we'd like to know about you, and enclosed it in this letter. Please fill it in and send it back next time you write. Can you believe we don't even know these things?"*

Christie looked at the list. It had all kinds of questions besides those Melanie had mentioned. Like: your favorite movie, female movie star, male singer, female singer, TV show, video, and food. Christie realized she didn't know those things about her friends, either. She'd have to make four lists and ask each of them to fill one out for her.

The phone rang downstairs and stopped when someone picked it up. After a few moments, when no one called for her, she let her shoulders sag. She should have known it wasn't for her. Who would want to talk to her, anyway?

Back home it would have been different. She got calls every night from someone. When it was Melanie, she could hardly get off the telephone. She hadn't talked to anyone on the phone since the move.

"Christie . . . telephone!" her mother called.

Startled, Christie dropped the pictures she had begun looking at and hurried to the top of the stairs. "I'll get it in the study!" Picking up the phone in the other room, she said, "Hello."

"Hi, Christie?"

"Yes."

"This is Phoebe. Eleanore, Nicki, and I were wondering if you'd like to go with us to the films this evening. There's a great flick on at the Strand. It's a comedy with the Stones in it."

"The Stones?"

"The Rolling Stones. Mick Jagger and his band."

Christie hesitated. One part of her was pleased that

somebody had finally called, the other part was frightened. In school all you had to do was keep your nose buried in your books and keep quiet. That way you didn't make an idiot of yourself. She didn't know the rules outside of school. Would she do the wrong things and get laughed at?

She took a deep breath. "What time are you going? I'll have to ask my parents if I can go, and ask my dad for a ride."

"Around seven. We'll meet you in front. Probably drop by the club after to see what's happening. Nicki always wants to because Connie goes there lots. You can call your mum and dad from there and have them pick you up."

"I hate to have to ask, Phoebe, but what's the club?"

"I guess you kids from the States might call it a teen center. You can dance or play Table Tennis and video games, if you'd like."

"What'll I wear?" Christie felt foolish having to ask such questions, but she didn't know, and she didn't want to be embarrassed.

"Certainly not your school uniform," Phoebe replied with a laugh. "Wear whatever you'd wear in the States when you went out with your chums."

"Give me your number, and I'll call you back," said Christie.

After she had hung up, Christie sat at her mother's desk, hugging the bear she had brought with her. Should she go or not? She could call Phoebe back and tell her she had plans she had forgotten about. After all, Phoebe had called at the last minute, so they hadn't been thinking for very long about asking her. Maybe they were hoping Christie already had something to do. So if Christie said she did, it could be what they wanted to hear.

"Well, are you going?"

Christie swiveled her chair around to see her mother standing in the doorway. Mrs. Winchell had a smile on her face.

In response to the puzzled look on Christie's face, her mother said, "Are you going to the movies with them? That nice young lady introduced herself when she called and said she and her friends wanted to ask you. You are going, aren't you?"

Christie was trapped.

CHAPTER

12

*C*hristie took a deep breath as her father pulled up to the curb in front of the Strand. Phoebe, Eleanore, and Nicki were waiting for her under the lighted marquee.

Nicki had on a short white skirt, a white blouse with black lettering on it, and a black vest. Long gold chains hung around her neck, and another chain circled her waist. Her hair had been moussed to stand in straight spikes. Christie had to admit she dressed even more wildly than Beth.

Phoebe was wearing black slacks and a white V-necked sweater with a green turtleneck under it. Her medium brown hair was pulled back away from her face. Eleanore was wearing a dark blue skirt and gray pullover that made her look mousy next to Nicki.

Christie was relieved to see that her light blue skirt and white blouse fit in with what they were wearing.

Phoebe waved when she saw Christie get out of the car.

"That Mick Jagger is bonkers," said Nicki as the four of them walked out of the theater after the show.

"I think the whole movie was daft," remarked Eleanore. "There was no sense to it at all. All they did was run around and make idiots of themselves."

"Everything doesn't have to make sense, Ellie," said Nicki. "You want everything to fit neatly in little boxes. That's not my way, believe me. *I* like things loose, so you can . . . what's it you Americans say, Christie?"

Christie shrugged. "Go with the flow?" she guessed.

"That's it!" said Nicki. "I like to go with the flow, if you know what I mean. My whole family's that way."

"Not mine," said Christie. "My mom hates to have anything out of place. That's why she has help at home."

"Your family has a daily, does it?" asked Nicki.

Christie drew a blank. "A daily?"

"She means a maid," explained Phoebe.

"Mrs. Coldwell comes in twice a week," answered Christie.

"I suppose she cleans your room, too," said Nicki.

"No, I do. But she works on the rest of the house."

"Pretty cushy," replied Nicki.

Christie felt heat rising in her face.

"Belt up, McAfee," said Phoebe. "Christie doesn't know you well enough for you to go poppin' off. Don't explain it to her, Christie. She'll just keep after you. Give her what for, and she'll leave you alone."

Nicki gave a little smirk.

"Here's the club," said Eleanore.

Christie looked at what seemed to be a plain old storefront. The windows were painted over so she couldn't see in. The sign over the door said MONTAGUE YOUTH CLUB in faded letters. Music came from inside.

The girls entered a large room with two Ping-Pong tables and several video games on one side. A jukebox and a dance floor filled in the center, and soda and snack machines lined the opposite wall. Three couples were dancing, and both Ping-Pong tables had hot contests going on.

The four girls found an empty booth.

"There's no one here," said Nicki with a pout.

"I'm surprised you say that." Eleanore nodded toward the vending machines.

"Well, how'd I miss him?" A broad smile brightened Nicki's face.

Christie turned to see. Three boys were getting sodas from the machines. One was short, with his hair combed back and caught in a rattail that hung over his shirt collar. The second was tall and thin, with a slightly hooked nose. She recognized the third one. It was the blond-haired boy from the bus.

"Fancy Connie's being here," said Nicki, running her fingers through her hair to make the spikes stand up.

"As if you didn't know." Phoebe laughed. "It's why you wanted to come to the club all along, isn't it?"

"I think you've got a spy at St. Regis, Nicki," teased Eleanore. "How else would you know his whereabouts all the time?"

"I bet Charlie Fenwick's the one she's been talking to," said Phoebe.

"Nicki's got a thing for Connie," Eleanore explained to Christie. "In case you couldn't tell."

Christie smiled. She could tell.

"Belt up!" hissed Nicki. "He's coming over."

Christie watched as the three boys headed their way. The blonde was the most interesting to her. He was slender, with square shoulders, and there was something special about the way he carried himself.

"Hi," he said. "Can we sit with you?"

His eyes came to rest on Christie's, and she felt her face heating up. Little tingles ran up and down her spine.

"Not at all," said Nicki, squeezing up against Eleanore to make room.

He slid in next to Christie, the tall boy dropped down next to Nicki, and the shorter one got a chair from a table.

Christie was surprised when she saw Nicki staring angrily at her. What's her problem? Christie wondered.

"My name's Conrad Farrell," said the blond boy to Christie. "Everybody calls me Connie. You ride our bus in the morning, don't you? What's your name?"

Christie had the feeling that the evening had just turned into a total disaster.

CHAPTER

13

"**I**'m Christie Winchell," said Christie, glancing at Nicki. She knew she was in trouble by the way Nicki was watching them.

"You go to St. Meg's with these birds, don't you?" asked Connie. "It's for cert' you don't care who you hang out with," he joked.

She smiled at him in spite of the dark looks Nicki was giving her. "We're in the same class at St. Meg's."

"Do I hear an American accent in your voice?"

The question surprised Christie. "I suppose . . . I never thought of myself as having any kind of accent, but now that I'm in England, I guess I probably do."

"Well, Miss Winchell with an accent, would you care to dance with me?"

She looked quickly at the other girls. Phoebe nodded encouragingly. Christie drew in a deep breath. "Okay."

The music was medium fast, and it was easy to pick up the rhythm. Other couples came out onto the floor, and soon Christie felt right at home. The style of dancing wasn't that different from what they did at the Wakeman Junior High dances, and Connie moved with a surprising grace most boys didn't have. He didn't take his eyes off Christie the entire time they were dancing. It made her feel a little self-conscious, but she was having fun.

The music ended, and when she turned to go back to the booth, Connie took her hand and stopped her. "Let's not quit now," he said. Christie could feel Nicki's eyes on them as they stood waiting.

"Who's your favorite rock group, Christie?" Connie asked.

"Brain Damage. They played at our school this year."

He raised his eyebrows. "Trevor Morgan's band? They're my favorites, too. They're from London, you know."

"Yes. My friends and I met him. He's a great person."

"I think so, too," said Connie. "I met him at one of the charity balls my mum puts on. If she has him again, I'll get you a ticket."

Christie couldn't believe her ears. "I'd love that," she said.

After they finished the next dance, they went back to the others.

"This here's Davey Hopper," Phoebe announced as Christie and Connie slid in the booth.

Christie said hello to the tall boy.

"And he's Charlie Fenwick," Phoebe said, indicating the boy with the rattail.

Christie smiled at him.

"And this is Christie Winchell. As Connie said, she's from the States."

The boys looked at Christie with interest.

Just then the music started again, and Nicki reached across the table and grabbed Connie's hand. "Come on, love, it's my turn to have a dance with you."

Charlie asked Eleanore to dance, and Davey wandered off, leaving Christie and Phoebe alone.

"I don't think Nicki likes me very much," Christie said.

"Oh, don't pay her any mind, Christie. She's not half as bad as she'd like you to think. As she says, things run in her family. Her older brother's twice as sarcastic as she is."

"She sure wasn't happy about my dancing with Connie."

"She has dreams about dating royalty, that's all."

"Royalty?"

Phoebe finished her soda. "Connie's in the royal bloodline somewhere."

Christie opened her eyes in surprise. "Is he a prince?"

"Oh, no." Phoebe laughed. "Nothing of the sort. His father does have some kind of fancy title, and his family lives in an elegant mansion, but you'd never know it the way Connie carries on. Connie's all right."

Now Christie understood Connie's comment about his mother's charity balls. "He and Nicki aren't going steady, are they?" she asked.

"No. Not that Nicki wouldn't like to. Oh, there's a couple of friends over there I want to say hello to," said Phoebe. "Why don't you come along and meet them?"

"I don't think so," answered Christie. "I'll just stay here, if you don't mind."

"It's up to you. I'll be back shortly."

Christie looked out onto the dance floor, where Connie and Nicki were dancing. No matter what Phoebe said, Christie was sure that Nicki didn't like her. And if one person in a group didn't like you, well . . . you were dead. There was no way Christie could be best friends with Phoebe and Eleanore and not Nicki. Nicki would think she was trying to break up their group.

Christie looked around the room. Spotting a pay phone, she grabbed her purse and went to call her parents for a ride.

After she finished making the call, she returned to the booth. Nicki and Connie were back. Nicki had her arm wrapped through his possessively, and Charlie was sitting between Eleanore and Phoebe.

"Hey, thanks a lot for asking me to come with you

guys," said Christie. "But I need to get home. I called my dad, and he'll be here in a minute to pick me up."

"Going home?" asked Eleanore, looking at her watch. "It's early."

"Well, I, uh, . . . I've got something that I have to do tomorrow. I've got to get up early."

"You don't really have to go," said Connie. "Call your folks, and tell them you made a mistake and want to stay longer."

"Oh, let her be," said Nicki. "She knows what she has to do."

"But . . ." started Eleanore. Christie saw Phoebe nudge Eleanore, and Eleanore didn't finish what she was going to say.

Later, in her room, Christie opened her desk drawer and took out the magic box. She needed it now. She reread each letter, leaving Chase's for last.

Instead of feeling better, she felt worse. She had been in London for four weeks now, and things weren't much better than when she first got here. She wished she could say something without having to think first whether it might sound strange to people here. And it seemed like she was forever asking what some word meant. And when was the last time she had actually laughed really hard? That was an easy one. It was the last time she was with The Fabulous Five.

Phoebe was nice, Christie had to admit. Eleanore

was all right, too. But neither of them was at all like Jana, or Katie, or Melanie, or Beth. And Nicki was like no one Christie had ever met. Christie didn't know if they could ever be friends.

Especially now. Nicki probably hated her because Connie had paid attention to her. As if it had been Christie's fault that Connie asked her to dance.

He was a good dancer, too. Christie couldn't help remembering the fluid way he moved around the floor, smiling at her all the time. She wondered if he had had to go to a school to learn how to do all the things princes and princesses did. Christie bet he had gone to dance school.

She took the paper clip off Chase's things and held up his picture. Connie's blond good looks were a sharp contrast to Chase's black hair and beautiful dark eyes. She bet that Chase was a better athlete than Connie. After all, Chase was a Junior Olympic swim champion.

Well, Nicki could keep her royal boyfriend. Christie had Chase. The only problem is, Christie reminded herself, that Chase is thousands of miles away.

There was one way to feel a little closer to him and to her other true blue friends. She opened up the middle drawer to her desk and took out her stationery. Maybe she'd even put some X's on the bottom of her letter to Chase.

CHAPTER

14

"Y ou guys aren't the only ones Christie's writing to," said Chase, waving an envelope in front of The Fabulous Five. He was standing at the end of their booth at Bumpers.

"What's that? A letter from Christie?" asked Melanie, reaching for it. "Let me see it."

"Oh, no, you don't." Chase held it high over his head. "It's a personal, private letter. It's meant for my eyes only."

"That's not fair," protested Beth. "We tell you what's in Christie's letters to us."

"And we gave you her address," joined in Melanie.

"You don't tell me *everything* she says," replied Chase. "But that's okay. I want you to know I appreciate that, but some of this is very personal. I'll read you the parts that aren't."

Dear Chase:

"That part's a *little* personal, but I threw it in because you've been so nice to me," he teased, ducking the napkin Beth threw at him.

I got your letter and was really glad to hear from you. I also got one from Melanie the same day.

Things are okay here. I think the thing I miss most, besides my friends, is the malls where we all used to hang out. They don't have malls here. They do have teen clubs, where you can go and listen to music and play Ping-Pong. I went to one tonight with some girls from school. It was all right.

"That's it," said Chase, folding the letter and putting it back into the envelope.

"What do you mean, *that's it?*" protested Katie. "That's not all she said."

"No it's not, but it's all I can read to you," declared Chase, looking embarrassed. "The rest is the personal stuff."

"Oh, no!" exclaimed Jana. "That letter's two pages long. That can't *all* be personal."

"Yes, it can, and it is," he replied, laughing.

"You're a rat, Chase Collins," said Melanie. "See if we ever do you any more favors."

"It really wouldn't interest you." He turned serious. "If it would, I'd let you read it." Sticking the letter in his back pocket, he turned and went to join Shane and Scott Daly by the jukebox.

"Maybe one of us can pick Chase's pocket," said Melanie. "The letter's sticking out of his pocket."

"Mel, you're impossible," said Beth. "If it has anything to do with love, you want in on it. By the way, I talked to Dekeisha after school and told her we'd save her a seat. Don't let anyone get that chair by you, Melanie."

"Remember our plan," said Jana.

"I appeal to her intelligent side," offered Katie.

"I talk to her about acting," added Beth.

"And I talk to her about boys," chimed in Melanie.

"And I'll show interest in anything else she wants to talk about," concluded Jana, smiling. "That way she'll know we like her and will want to hang out with us."

"Shh," said Beth softly. "She just came in."

Suddenly Alexis Duvall was standing in front of them with a soda and an order of fries. "Hi, guys," she said cheerfully as she slid into the empty chair. "Thanks for saving me a seat."

The Fabulous Five looked quickly at each other.

"Oh, uh . . . sure," said Jana, glancing in Dekeisha's direction.

Alexis smiled and ate a french fry.

Dekeisha saw them and headed in their direction.

"Hi," said the tall black girl. "I thought you guys were going to save a seat for me."

"Uh, we meant to," answered Beth. "Is there a spare chair at another table that we can get?" She and Melanie stood up and looked around.

Alexis helped look for a chair, too.

"I don't see any," said Dekeisha.

"Here, I'll share," said Jana, giving up half of hers.

"Well . . ." Katie glanced at Alexis and then Dekeisha. "How's your PEAK class going, Dekeisha? Since Christie left, we haven't heard much about what's going on in it."

"It's okay," answered Dekeisha. "Mr. Dracovitch has us studying dinosaurs. They're interesting."

"Oh, yeah, dinosaurs. I know something about them," said Katie confidently. "They lived thousands of years ago."

"More like millions of years ago," replied Dekeisha.

"And they were all huge," continued Katie brightly.

"Some of them were," Dekeisha explained. "But did you know that some of them were as small as chickens?"

"No." Katie looked surprised. "But I know they were fierce. Can you imagine all those animals growling and fighting each other day and night? It must have been horrible. It's a wonder they lasted as long as they did."

"Most of them were vegetarians," corrected Dekeisha. "Even the ones that were sixty or seventy feet long ate plants, so I don't imagine they fought much. Mr. Dracovitch told us that only about one out of every twenty were meat eaters."

"Is that right?" said Katie, looking surprised again.

"That shows how much of a dinosaur expert you are, Katie." Alexis laughed.

Beth tried a different tack. "I was wondering, Dekeisha, have you ever thought about joining Drama Club?"

"No, I haven't."

"Well, I think you ought to. That Bill Cosby skit that you did at the great TV turnoff assembly was a riot."

Alexis was looking back and forth between Beth and Dekeisha as they talked. A frown was growing on her face. "What's going on?" she asked.

Beth raised her eyebrows. "We're just talking."

"Yeah. With Dekeisha. Excuse me, Dekeisha. It's nothing against you, but it's like I'm not here. Were you saving this seat for her and not me?" she said, looking from one Fabulous Five member to another.

"Uh . . . we just weren't thinking," said Jana. "We should have saved two seats."

"Are you guys mad at me?" asked Alexis, her voice rising. "I've been going places with you guys for the last couple of weeks. All of a sudden now I feel as if I'm invisible."

Other kids were starting to turn and listen. Laura McCall had a smirk on her face as she and Melissa McConnell moved closer.

"Oh, no!" Jana assured Alexis. "Katie and Beth were just asking Dekeisha a couple of questions."

"What about saving the seat? Was it for Dekeisha or me?"

"Both," replied Melanie. "Yeah, that's right. We were saving it for both of you. We just miscounted."

"Miscounted?" said Alexis, an amazed look on her face. "Well, *excuuuse* me. I'll see you guys around." She picked up her fries and soda and marched off.

The Fabulous Five stared at each other.

"I think I'll go talk to Don," said Dekeisha softly. She got up and left them by themselves.

CHAPTER

15

"**W**ow! We blew it that time," said Jana as the four of them walked to Katie's house. "Why in the world didn't we think about how Alexis might feel when we started asking Dekeisha to hang out with us instead of her?"

"Yeah. She may never speak to us again," said Melanie.

"We've got to apologize," Beth told them. "Maybe she's not the right person to be in The Fabulous Five, but we don't want her to be angry with us, either."

They walked along in silence for a few minutes, before Katie said, "I didn't score any points with Dekeisha, either. I really thought I knew something about dinosaurs. Were there really chicken-size dinosaurs, or was she kidding me?"

"If Dekeisha says there were, I'm sure there were," said Jana.

"If they were chicken-size, do you suppose cavemen ate Kentucky Fried dinosaur?" asked Beth, chuckling.

"Or fried dinosaur eggs and bacon for breakfast?" asked Melanie.

"Funny," said Katie sarcastically. "But what about Dekeisha? Do you think she's angry at us, too?"

"I don't think so," replied Beth.

"Me, either," agreed Jana. "There's no reason for her to feel any differently toward us. I just think we have to straighten things out with Alexis. We'll tell her we were talking to Dekeisha and said we'd save a seat for her at Bumpers. We just forgot about Alexis, and that's the truth. We really didn't want to make her feel bad."

"And did you notice that nasty Laura McCall listening to every word?" said Melanie. "Why is it that every time something goes wrong for us, she's there?"

They turned into the walkway to Katie's house.

"Mom! I'm home," called Katie as they entered the front door.

Katie's mother came out of her office. "Hi, sweetheart. Hi, girls. Katie, there's a letter for you, from Christie, on the kitchen counter."

The four girls charged down the hallway into the kitchen.

"I get to open it!" shouted Katie. "You guys got to open the other ones."

"Well, hurry," said Melanie, bouncing up and down.

Katie found the letter and tore it open. With the other three looking over her shoulder, she read:

Hi, Katie:

You're last but definitely not least! You've got to be-lieve that. I love you all the same. I tell that to my bears every night before I go to bed, too.

I got a letter from Chase today. It was really nice. I think he likes me. He told me the same things you did, that he has been awfully good. Why, oh why, did things have to turn out the way they did, with me here and him there? It's almost as bad as you guys being there and me here.

I'm going to write him as soon as I finish this letter to you, Katie. If I can get the courage, I may tell him how much I like him.

Guess what! I met royalty. The other night some girls asked me to go to a teen club with them, and we met this guy named Connie Farrell. His real name is Conrad. Phoebe told me that Connie's family is related to the queen a bunch of times removed. He also knows Trevor Morgan personally. He told me he'd get me a ticket the next time Trevor comes to one of his mother's charity balls. Isn't that fantastic?

Hey, thanks for the pictures and other stuff. I filled out the list of my favorite things that you sent. I've made up my own lists for you guys to fill out. They've got the same things you had on yours, plus some other things, like what was the funniest thing that ever happened to us, what was the most embarrassing thing, what was

the scariest thing, and what was the weirdest thing that
ever happened to us. Fill them out and send them back,
okay? I'll put them in my magic box, where I keep ev-
erything I get from you.
    There's not much more to say, so I'll close for now.
Keep the cards and letters coming.
Love you,
    Christie

"Gee." Beth sank into a kitchen chair. "Christie met
real royalty."

"I wonder if she said anything about meeting Connie Farrell in her letter to Chase," said Melanie.

Katie shook her head. "Fat chance. Would you tell
Shane if you met some great new guy?"

"Definitely not," agreed Melanie.

Jana sat down. "So what are we going to do about
Alexis and Dekeisha?"

"I think your idea to tell Alexis the truth was a terrific one," said Beth. "Why don't *you* talk to her?"

"You're a rat," said Jana.

"I'm just kidding," replied Beth. "I think we should
all explain to Alexis what happened. That way she'll
know we're sincere. We can each call her after supper."

"Good idea," chimed in Melanie. "And a couple of
us should call Dekeisha, too. If she asks what happened at Bumpers, we tell her the truth, too. We just
forgot to save Alexis a seat."

"Right," said Katie. "But I've got one request."

The other girls waited to hear what it was.

"I'd like for someone else to take over the job of talking to Dekeisha about intellectual things. I've goofed too much already." Everyone laughed.

"I'll talk to her some more about Drama Club," volunteered Beth. "I think she really is interested in joining, and I'd like to convince her to do it. She could be a great actress."

"Terrific," said Jana. "I think we should *all* just be ourselves with Dekeisha. Making believe we're something we aren't only gets us in trouble."

Jana was humming to herself when she got home. It looked as if The Fabulous Five would be able to straighten things out between them and Alexis. And Jana really liked Dekeisha. She just might be the one to take Christie's place in the group.

Her mother was already home from her job at the newspaper when Jana walked into the kitchen. "Hi, sweetheart. You look happy. Did you have a good day?"

"I thought for a while it was going to be a real bummer," answered Jana, smiling. "But it turned out okay."

She raised the lid on the cookie jar and looked in. "Katie got a letter from Christie today. So did Chase Collins. Christie said she met a boy who's a distant relative of the queen."

"I'm impressed," said Jana's mother, thumbing through a recipe book.

Just then the phone rang. Jana swallowed her bite of cookie and answered it.

"Hello," she said cheerfully.

"Jana, this is Funny." She sounded very serious. "I thought you ought to know what Laura's telling everybody."

Jana froze. "What?"

"She's telling everybody you guys are *recruiting* for a new member for The Fabulous Five."

"*Recruiting for a new member?*"

"That's right. She says she believes you were going to ask Alexis to join, but somebody must have *blacklisted* her. Now you're thinking about Dekeisha. Jana . . ."

Jana was almost too stunned to respond. "Yes."

"Is it true?"

CHAPTER

16

*M*ovement outside Christie's window caught her attention. The lady with the cat had come out onto her porch. She had shed her usual raincoat for a sweater. The cat slipped past the lady's legs and down the stairs. Falling on its back, it rubbed itself luxuriously against the rough pave-stone walk.

Christie smiled at the cat's playfulness. For the first time since she had started watching, it was acting like a kitten. Even the woman seemed livelier without the drab raincoat and scarf to hide her. Christie closed the book she was studying from and trotted down the stairs.

"How long till dinner, Mom?"

"Oh, half an hour," responded Mrs. Winchell, closing the oven door.

"I'll be out back," Christie called over her shoulder just before the door slammed behind her.

Plunking herself down on the top step, she looked around the courtyard. It surprised her to realize that she had seen it only from the windows of their apartment . . . or flat, as Phoebe and Eleanore called it.

The yard was more spacious than it had appeared. All four sides were pretty much the same, with red brick walls, and windows and doors opening onto the yard. The Winchells' back door was the only one that didn't have potted plants sitting or hanging around it. The walkway around the perimeter of the court connected all the back doors, and in the center was a lone tree, with two benches under it. The smells that wafted outside told Christie that other families were preparing their evening meals, too.

"Meooow!"

Christie looked down at the small visitor that had approached unnoticed. The brown tabby cat looked up at her and mouthed a second, but silent, greeting. Christie stretched out her hand and wiggled her fingers, and the cat walked over to her, stopping to sniff a leaf on the way.

"Nice kitty," said Christie as it rubbed up against her legs.

"My Agatha isn't pulling her monkey tricks on you, is she?" called the lady. "Send her running if she is."

"Oh, no, ma'am," Christie called back. "She's being very nice."

Christie scratched Agatha, who humped her back

like a tiny camel. Picking the cat up, Christie walked over to its owner.

"A friend of mine has a pet named Agatha," said Christie. "Only it's a huge Old English sheepdog."

The lady looked up from weeding her plants. Her face was pale, as if she hadn't been in the sun enough, but her skin was surprisingly smooth for someone of her age. Her blue eyes were bright behind old-fashioned wire-rimmed glasses. Christie's grandma wore glasses like hers.

"I suspect the two animals aren't related," the woman said.

Christie laughed. "No, I don't think so. You have beautiful flowers."

There was no reply.

Christie stroked the cat and wondered if she should say anything else or go about her business. She wasn't sure if the woman wanted to be friendly.

"Do you do child-minding?" asked the lady as she snipped flowers and made them into a bouquet.

"You mean do I baby-sit?" asked Christie, unsure of what she meant.

"Whatever you want to call it," replied the woman. "You're new here, I know. Most girls your age like to earn a little spending money. There's a young couple in number fifty-two." She indicated a door with a nod of her head. "They've got a little daughter. The mum works, and they need someone to tend her some evenings. They might hire you."

"Oh," said Christie. She thought for a moment. "I

am going to need money to buy birthday presents for my friends at home. A child-minding job would sure help."

"I'll say something to them for you. Their name is Fitzhugh. What should I say yours is?"

"Christie Winchell."

"Well, Christie Winchell, take these flowers to your mum. Tell them it's a little present from Maude Mansfield and Agatha, the cat."

"Oh, thank you!" exclaimed Christie. "They're beautiful."

The lady smiled warmly at her and continued pruning her plants.

"Where'd the flowers come from?" asked Mr. Winchell at the supper table. "They're gorgeous."

"They were given to Christie by one of our neighbors," answered his wife.

"Her name's Mrs. Mansfield," offered Christie. "She lives in our court, and they're from her garden. She's awfully nice."

"I hereby salute Christie for being the first person to meet someone in the courtyard." Her father raised his water glass.

"I've been thinking about that very subject," said Christie's mother. "We've all been so busy getting settled, we haven't taken time to meet our neighbors. Our belongings should be getting here from the States any day now. When they arrive and I can get out our dishes, I think we should have an open house. We can invite all the people from Queen's Pudding Square."

"Excellent idea," said Mr. Winchell. "We'll help, won't we, Christie?"

"You're darn right you two will help," said his wife, laughing. "I'm counting on that. And we'll have Mrs. Coldwell in to help clean, too."

"I'll fill out the invitations," volunteered Christie.

"And clean your room and help with the snacks," added her mother.

Later that evening as Christie was getting ready for bed, the phone rang.

Her father stuck his head out of the study and called down the hall to her. "It's for you, Christie. You can take it in here if you want, but it's a boy, so you might want to take it downstairs, where you can have some privacy."

Puzzled, Christie took his advice and went downstairs.

"Hello."

"Hi, Christie. This is Connie Farrell. We met the other night at the club."

"Oh, yes. I remember," she responded.

"I just called to chat," he said. "How is it going at school?"

"Okay. I'm still getting used to things. Going to an all-girls school is kind of strange, and some other things are different, too, but I'm managing."

"Even though the English and Americans are a lot

alike, I'm sure we still take a bit of getting used to," said Connie.

"It's kind of like looking in a mirror at a carnival," said Christie. "Your mind tells you things are one way, and they turn out to be another way." She heard his laughter at the other end of the line.

"Would you like to go to the cinema with me this Friday?" he asked.

She hadn't expected the question, and hesitated. What about Chase? Would she have to tell him she had a date with someone else? And what if Nicki found out that she had gone to a movie with Connie? Christie thought she knew the answer to that. Nicki would be furious. But still, it did sound like fun. She needed time to think.

"Uh . . . I don't know," said Christie.

"Is there another cove?"

"Cove?"

He chuckled. "Sorry. Cove's slang for a guy. Do you have a boyfriend?"

Christie could feel herself turning red. "Kind of."

"Is he here or back in the States?"

"Back in the States."

"Well, then he hardly counts at all," replied Connie cheerfully. "If he's there and I'm here, I've got the upper hand now, haven't I?"

"Well, I . . . uh . . ."

"I don't mean to be pushy, but you might as well agree to go. I'll keep asking until you do."

"I don't know," Christie fumbled. "Not this week-end."

"At least you didn't say no," said Connie. "I'll keep trying until you say yes."

After he had hung up, Christie went back to her room. She took her box from the desk drawer and climbed onto her bed. She took out Chase's things.

Her mind was spinning. Connie seemed nice, but her heart still skipped a beat every time she thought of Chase or looked at his picture. Was it being untrue to Chase to have a friendly date with Connie? Could she and Connie just be friends? She remembered the time she had broken off with Jon Smith and tried to continue to be friends. It had been hard.

Then there was Nicki. Things were shaky enough between the two of them as it was. If she made an enemy of Nicki by dating Connie, it would probably ruin any chance she had of being friends with Phoebe and Eleanore. After all, they were Nicki's friends first.

Christie let out a big sigh and flopped back on her bed. It was all so confusing.

She reached out and pulled the five bears into her arms. If only Jana, Katie, Beth, and Melanie were around to help her solve her problems. They would make everything all right. They always did.

CHAPTER

17

"*M*iss Winchell, would you see me after class?" said Miss Woolsey.

A sudden flash of anxiety ran through Christie. She searched her memory. What could she have done wrong that Miss Woolsey would want to talk to her about? Could she be failing some subject? She had thought she was doing her homework correctly. Had one of her teachers given her a bad report? Had she broken some rule? By the time the bell rang, Christie was almost beside herself with worry.

Christie walked timidly to the teacher's desk and stood waiting quietly, hands clasped in front of her, while Miss Woolsey finished filling in a report. She could feel moisture gathering in the palms of her hands.

Finally, Miss Woolsey looked at Christie over her

glasses. The teacher's eyes started at Christie's feet and worked their way up to the top of her head. Christie felt like a bug being examined under a microscope. She braced herself for the worst.

"Miss Winchell," said the teacher firmly.

"Yes, Miss Woolsey," Christie responded as politely as she could.

"You've been with us a few weeks now, and as is my policy with new students, I've been following your progress closely. I've made contact with each of your other mistresses to find out how you are doing in your subjects and about your deportment. I feel it's my responsibility to St. Margaret's, your parents, and you to do so."

Christie forced back the swallow that was rising in her throat and tried not to blink.

"I have found that you are doing exceedingly well in all your subjects," continued Miss Woolsey, "and the other mistresses report your conduct as excellent."

Christie felt her knees go weak with relief.

The teacher looked her in the eyes. "That is exactly the kind of report I *expect* on each of my students," she said matter-of-factly. "So don't feel proud."

"Yes, ma'am," said Christie. "I won't."

"One other thing," said the teacher. "How are you getting along with your classmates?"

"Oh . . . fine," answered Christie.

Miss Woolsey looked at her for a moment before saying, "Very well, you are dismissed."

Feeling as if she had just escaped a death penalty, Christie headed for the door.

"Miss Winchell." Miss Woolsey's voice stopped her before she could leave. "Keep up the good work."

"Yes, ma'am. I'll try," answered Christie. In spite of herself, she broke out into a big grin. She thought she saw the tiniest smile at the corners of the teacher's mouth, too.

Christie was feeling good when lunchtime came. Miss Woolsey was scary, but she had been nice to Christie in her own way.

As they came through the serving line together, Eleanore advised Christie that the sausages and mashed potatoes that were being served were called bangers and mash.

"Bangers and mash," Christie thought to herself. She couldn't wait to tell The Fabulous Five this newest British phrase. They would love it.

"Aren't you the lucky one," a girl named Becca said to Christie as she took a seat next to her.

"Why?" asked Christie. She wondered if somehow Becca knew about the praise she had gotten from Miss Woolsey.

"I saw Charlie Fenwick on my bus this morning, and he said that Connie Farrell has taken a liking to you."

"Wow!" exclaimed a girl named Denise. "You really must rate."

Christie blushed and glanced at Nicki. She was staring at her.

"I just met him when Phoebe, Nicki, Eleanore, and

I were at the Montague Teen Club," Christie explained. "I haven't seen him since," she added for Nicki's benefit.

"Charlie said Connie was going to ring you up for a date," Becca went on.

Christie started to panic. How could she lie and say he hadn't called?

"I'd just die if Connie rang me up," said Denise. "He's gorgeous."

Christie decided the best thing to do was to keep her mouth shut and not say anything about Connie unless she was asked a direct question. She couldn't help being aware of Nicki watching her as she ate her bangers and mash.

"Does he really live in a mansion?" asked a small, studious-looking girl.

"Nicki's been in it, haven't you?" said Eleanore.

Everyone turned to hear Nicki's response.

"It's a mansion, all right," answered Nicki. "It's full of beautiful old furniture, and it's got chandeliers that look like they're made out of the queen's diamonds, they sparkle so bright. And there are all these paintings of his ancestors, in gold frames on the walls and going up the stairway."

Christie saw a dreamy look come into Nicki's eyes.

"You'd go out with Connie if he asked you, wouldn't you, Christie?" asked Denise. "You'd be a fool not to."

"I'm sure I'd say no," Christie replied truthfully. That was exactly what she had done. "I've got a boyfriend in the United States."

"Sooner or later you'd say yes to him," said Becca. "After all, you're not going back to the States soon."

Christie took a bite of sausage and didn't reply. Nicki was still watching her.

"You got a letter from Katie," Christie's mother greeted her after school.

"Where? Where?" said Christie. She found the stack of mail and excitedly flipped through the magazines and letters.

"A Mrs. Fitzhugh called, Christie," said her mother. "She said that Mrs. Mansfield had given her your name and said you might baby-sit. She wants you to call. The number's on my grocery pad."

"Oh, great. I'll call her as soon as I read my letter from Katie." Christie picked up her books and went up to her room.

Dear Christie:

It was great to hear from you. As you must know, we all share your letters.

Chase showed us a letter he got from you. That's all he did was show it to us, though. He said it was full of personal things, and it made us want to know more about what you said to him. Melanie especially wanted to know; she almost couldn't stand not knowing what was in it.

Wow! You've met royalty. Everyone wants to know more about Connie. Is he cute? Is he rich? Melanie wants you to tell us as soon as he asks you for a date. And everyone says to say hi to Trevor Morgan if you get to see him. You're sooo lucky.

We've had some trouble here. Alexis is mad at us because we asked Dekeisha to sit with us and we forgot to ask her.

And Laura is at it again. She's telling everyone that we're interviewing people to take your place in The Fabulous Five. We aren't really. No one could take your place. We're just used to there being five of us instead of four, and we're trying to find someone that fits in. It's not our fault no one lives up to you.

Here are the lists of questions you asked us to answer. Isn't this fun? We didn't realize how much we didn't know about our best friends until we started doing this.

We've given each other lists just like the ones we sent you. Now we've got some different questions. Do you remember when you met each of us? What were you doing then? Why did you pick each of us for your best friend? You answer those questions, and we will, too, and send them to you.

Write soon.

Love,
Katie

Christie looked the questions over. She decided to take her time answering them, and she tucked the letter into her magic box.

So her friends thought she was lucky? It was true, she was starting to know a few people, although not nearly as many as she knew back home. But she still didn't have any special friends. On top of that she was trying to avoid having trouble with one girl over a boy.

The thing that confused her the most was what to do about Chase. She liked him so much. But did it make sense to keep caring for him? Should she continue to write to him and tell him she liked him? If only she had her Fabulous Five friends with her so they could help her think this all out. Writing letters to them about it wasn't the same.

It *had* felt good to have Miss Woolsey tell her in her stern way that she thought Christie was doing well in school.

Christie looked at her reflection in the wardrobe mirror and pretended to look over eyeglasses the way Miss Woolsey did.

Suddenly Christie remembered Mrs. Fitzhugh and went into the study to call her.

"Hello," answered a woman in a pleasant-sounding voice.

"Hello, Mrs. Fitzhugh. This is Christie Winchell. My mother said you called about my minding your baby."

"Oh, yes, dear. Walter and I frequently have need of someone. Would you have time later this evening to come visit and meet our Jenny?"

"Yes, ma'am."

"Good. When it's convenient, but before eight, please, drop by. Eight's when Jenny goes down."

"I'll be there," said Christie cheerily.

CHAPTER

18

"Laura McCall, you had better stop telling lies about us!" Jana stood with her hands on her hips and her feet spread wide. Her face was flushed with anger. They were at the school fence, and Katie, Melanie, and Beth were lined up behind her. Melissa, Tammy, and Funny were with Laura.

"Who says I'm telling lies about you?" retorted Laura, squinting at Jana.

"It's all over school that you're saying we're trying to recruit somebody for The Fabulous Five," said Beth. "It's not true."

"Oh? Isn't it?" asked Melissa. She had one eyebrow arched and looked smug. "Well, how come you stopped asking Alexis to do things with you and

135

started asking Dekeisha? Didn't Alexis want to join The Fabulous Five?"

"We didn't *ask* Alexis to join The Fabulous Five," shot back Jana.

"Just because we asked Dekeisha to do some things with us doesn't mean we don't like Alexis," joined in Katie.

"Well, I heard Alexis was upset because you didn't save her a seat," said Laura. "And because you ignored her when Dekeisha was sitting with you."

"We explained that to Alexis," said Beth. "And besides, it's none of your business, Laura. Why don't you just stay out of our lives?"

"Gladly," snapped Laura, spinning on her heel and stomping off with the other members of The Fantastic Foursome behind her.

"Alexis *is* our friend," said Jana. "There's no reason we can't ask her and Dekeisha both to hang out with us."

"That way we can show we're interested in both of them, and no one will believe Laura's lies," added Beth.

After they had settled down, Melanie turned to Katie. "How much money do we have in our treasury now?"

"I counted it last night. We've got twenty-one dollars and forty-five cents. Almost enough to call Christie."

"All right!" said Jana. "I know Mom will let me have an advance on my allowance for such a good cause."

"Me, too," said Beth. "We'll have more than enough. I can't wait!"

"Dekeisha! Over here," called Melanie. "We saved you a seat."

Dekeisha picked up her lunch tray and headed for the table where The Fabulous Five were seated.

"Remember, show her we're interested in her," whispered Melanie. "But be natural."

"And leave space for Alexis," warned Katie.

"Hi, guys," said Dekeisha, scooting into the spot they had saved for her.

"How's everything, Dekeisha?" asked Jana.

"Fine."

"I just love your sweater," said Beth. "I wish I had one like it. Where'd you get it?"

"Mom and I went shopping Saturday at Birnbaum's, and she bought it for me."

"How are you and Don Petry getting along?" asked Jana.

"Will you promise not to tell if I let you in on a secret?" asked Dekeisha. She looked slightly embarrassed.

"We promise." Melanie crossed her heart. "I like secrets. Tell us quick."

"I think Don's going to ask me to go steady."

"Super!" cried Melanie. "When?"

Dekeisha shrugged her shoulders and grinned. "I don't know. Maybe this weekend."

"Excuse me, Dekeisha," said Katie, "but there's Alexis. Hey, Alexis! Over here."

"Hi," said Alexis. "Do you have room for me? I can sit someplace else if you don't."

"We saved you a spot," said Beth, squeezing over next to Melanie.

"Thanks!" Alexis smiled and worked her way into the crowded seat.

"How is everything?" asked Jana.

"Fine," answered Alexis.

"I like your blouse," said Beth. "I wish I had one like it. Where'd you get it?"

As Alexis was answering Beth, Katie said to Dekeisha, "Those chicken-size dinosaurs we were talking about, did they actually look like chickens?"

"I doubt it," answered Dekeisha. "The archaeologists think they looked like regular dinosaurs, only tiny."

"How are you and Bill Soliday getting along, Alexis?" asked Jana.

"He asked me to go to the movies Friday. I think he likes me."

"Do you think he'll ask you to go steady?" asked Melanie.

Dekeisha looked puzzled at their conversation.

"I don't know," replied Alexis. "Maybe. Hey, Bill's sitting over there with Melinda and Marcie. Do you guys mind if I go sit with them so I can protect my interests?"

They laughed and shook their heads.

After she left, The Fabulous Five turned their attention back to Dekeisha. They asked her so many questions, she didn't have time to eat her lunch. When the bell rang, she had to gulp down the rest of her food.

As they left the tray return, Dekeisha stopped Katie. "Can I see you a minute, Katie? Over there, where we can talk in private." Dekeisha moved toward the corner of the room. Taking a deep breath, she said, "You know the rumors about you guys looking for a replacement for Christie?"

"We told you that it was Laura that was saying those things," said Katie.

"I know, and I believe that. But I wonder . . . you know I like you, Beth, Jana, and Melanie a lot, don't you?"

Katie nodded, wondering what Dekeisha was trying to say.

"When we were sitting at the table, it seemed like you guys were working awfully hard to find interesting things to talk to Alexis and me about. You should have heard yourselves. You were asking Alexis exactly the same questions you asked me when I first sat down with you."

"We were?"

"And when I got to thinking about it, I remembered your trying to find things to talk to me about the other day. That's when we talked about dinosaurs. You aren't *really* that interested in dinosaurs, are you?"

Katie shrugged. "Well, kind of."

Dekeisha grinned at her. "But not *that* much, right?"

Katie gave Dekeisha a sheepish smile. "Well, maybe not."

"See? You guys know that everybody likes you," she continued. "Well, maybe not Laura and her clique so much," Dekeisha corrected herself. "But you don't have to work so hard to get Alexis and me to like you. We already do. I thought you knew that. Can't we just go back to being friends the way we were? It was just, I don't know . . . it was just kind of a natural way of being friends."

Katie looked Dekeisha in the eyes. Every word she'd said made sense. "Thanks, Dekeisha. You really are a friend."

After Dekeisha had gone, Katie sat down on the corner of the nearest bench. She was glad everyone had left the cafeteria. She needed a few minutes to think.

Dekeisha's words had made something suddenly clear. It was as if the sun had come out from behind a cloud. Why hadn't she or her friends understood sooner? They had spent all this time doing the wrong things. Maybe they all missed Christie so much, they weren't thinking. Whatever the reason, they needed to have another meeting of The Fabulous Five and get back on the right track.

Katie opened her notebook to a back page where she had written down the others' class schedules. She had next period with Jana. She'd talk to her then.

CHAPTER

19

"**I** feel like an idiot," groaned Jana.

"Me, too," agreed Beth, throwing her arms out and flopping back on Katie's bed. "Deep down we knew what we were doing, but we refused to think of it as recruiting."

"I don't think we should feel all that bad," Melanie said, frowning. "Maybe we didn't do everything right, but it was because our hearts were in it more than our heads."

Katie made a face. "I think you're right, Mel. But it kills me to think that Laura McCall saw what was happening before we did."

"We've been trying to force things to be the way they were before Christie left," said Jana. "We've been doing it all along. First we didn't want to let go of

Christie, even though she's thousands of miles away. Then we tried to make The Fabulous Five like it was when she was with us. That wasn't fair to Alexis or Dekeisha."

"I'm not sure it was fair to Christie, either," added Beth.

"Can you imagine? We thought Dekeisha might be a good Fabulous Five member because she's smart like Christie." Katie shook her head. "Bells and whistles should have gone off when we started looking at people because of how much they were like Christie."

Jana got up from her chair, pulled a tissue out of a box, and blew her nose. "Dekeisha was right when she said things had been natural between us and her before. If we find someone who fits in *naturally* with The Fabulous Five, we'll know it. If we don't, we don't. There's nothing wrong with just the four of us being best friends."

Beth popped upright with a grin on her face. "That's right, there isn't. We're still best friends, so let's have a party and celebrate!"

The others looked at her questioningly.

"A party?" asked Melanie. "What kind of party?"

"I don't know," answered Beth. "What about a . . . a . . . *telephone party*!"

"A telephone party?" the other three repeated in unison.

"Yeah," said Beth, jumping off the bed excitedly. "I just got this fantastic, stupendous, colossal, magnificent idea. We can finish getting enough money to call Christie, right?"

"Easy," answered Katie.

"Like Dekeisha said, other kids are Christie's friends, too. Instead of keeping her to ourselves, why don't we see if other kids want to be in on the phone call?"

"We'll only have enough money for a half hour," said Melanie. "How could everyone talk to her?"

"A speaker phone!" said Beth, looking triumphant. "Doesn't your mother have a speaker phone in her office, Katie?"

"Yes, she does. She uses it so she can have her hands free to make notes when she's interviewing someone. But her office isn't big enough to get a lot of kids into."

"What if we borrowed her speaker phone and took it to Bumpers? Mr. Matson has a phone by his cash register. I bet he'd let us plug your mother's phone in there so everyone could hear and talk to Christie."

"Especially when we tell him we'll pay for the call!" said Melanie, jumping up and grabbing Beth's hands. "Beth, that's an *unbelievable* idea!"

The two of them danced around in a circle, singing, "*We're gonna have a party! We're gonna have a party!*"

"We've got to make plans," said Jana. "We have to write to Christie and tell her when we're going to call."

"I'll tell her about it," said Katie.

"If you're going to write her, Katie, does anyone have any pictures or any more questions to ask her?"

asked Melanie. "It's kind of fun writing down all these things about our friendship."

"I've got an idea," offered Jana. "How about predictions for the future? Like, 'What do you think is going to happen to me when I'm grown up?'"

"Well, you're going to marry Randy Kirwan for one thing," answered Beth.

"I think you're going to be a social worker," said Katie. "You're so good with people."

"Or a teacher," chimed in Melanie.

"We all know Katie's going to be a judge," said Jana.

"What about me?" asked Melanie. "What are your predictions for me?"

"You're definitely going to marry," answered Beth. "Maybe two or three guys at one time, if you can get away with it."

Melanie stuck her tongue out at Beth.

"You know what?" said Katie. "I've got another good idea."

The others turned to listen.

"We've been collecting all this interesting stuff about each other, like what we've done together that's been fun, what we like about each other, who our favorite singers are, what our favorite songs are, and why we picked each other for best friends. Why don't we make friendship books?"

"Friendship books?" asked Beth.

"Yeah," replied Katie, getting excited. "Let's each of us put together a book about all the things we know about each other."

"We could put our class pictures in it, too," said Melanie.

"And pictures of us doing fun things together," suggested Jana. "It's a great idea. I want a book about each of you for my very own."

"Me, too," said Beth. "That would be even more fun."

"I'll get some paper and pencils, and we'll start making them," said Katie. "Let's each make one for Christie, too. She'll love it."

"And we'll ask her to make one about her for each of us," said Melanie.

Soon The Fabulous Five were hard at work around Katie's kitchen table making friendship books.

CHAPTER

20

CHAPTER

20

Christie knocked on the rear door of the Fitzhughs' flat. The tall, slender woman who opened it looked as if she could be a fashion model. It wasn't because she was especially beautiful, but more because of her slender build and the immaculate way she was dressed. Her blond hair was cut short and very stylish.

"You're Christie? I'm Martha. Please, come in."

A man sitting at the kitchen table working on papers looked up at her over a pair of half eyeglasses. He had on a white dress shirt and bow tie and looked as if he would be uncomfortable in anything else.

"This is Mr. Fitzhugh, Christie. Walter, this is Christie Winchell from across the court."

"How do you do?" said her husband.

"Fine, thanks," answered Christie.

"Let's go where we won't bother Mr. Fitzhugh and his figures," said his wife.

Christie followed Mrs. Fitzhugh through the kitchen, down the long side hallway, and into the living room at the front of the apartment. If she hadn't known better, she would have thought she was in her own home. It was laid out just like the Winchells', and the furnishings were similar.

"Do sit down," said Mrs. Fitzhugh.

As Christie sat, she glanced around, and was surprised to see that there were no toys anywhere in the room. The apartment was just as immaculate as the Fitzhughs were. Was it possible that a child really lived here? From the look of things, little Jenny must be just like her mother. Christie imagined a perfect little girl dressed in a frilly starched dress with bows in her hair, sitting quietly with her hands folded in her lap. Christie decided that baby-sitting the Fitzhughs' child was probably going to be easy but boring.

"Mrs. Mansfield told me that you'd like a job minding children. I assume you have experience."

"Christie nodded. Suddenly she had a strange feeling that something was touching the backs of her legs. She moved her feet, and said, "I minded children lots before we moved. It's the way I earned extra money."

"That's exemplary of you," said Mrs. Fitzhugh. "What age children have you minded?"

"Oh, I've sat with kids that were as young as a year old," answered Christie.

"*Grrrr.*"

Christie jerked her legs at the sound of an animal under her chair.

"Jenny, come out from under there!" commanded Mrs. Fitzhugh.

"*Woof! Woof!*"

"She thinks she's a dog." Mrs. Fitzhugh had a tone of exasperation in her voice. She reached down and pulled a little girl out from under Christie's chair. The child's face was round and rosy, and her eyes were beaming. Her face was flushed with mischief. Instead of the clean and starched dress Christie had envisioned, her clothes were wrinkled, and she had smudges on her knees from crawling on the floor.

"*Ruff! Ruff!*" barked the child.

"Jenny, stop that! I'm sorry if she startled you, Christie. Jenny's three, and sometimes she can be incorrigible. Jenny, say hello to Christie, like a good girl."

"*Ruff!*" said Jenny.

Christie put her hand over her mouth to keep from laughing.

"Why don't we go upstairs, Jenny, and show Christie your room?"

Jenny ran on all fours into the hall and up the stairs.

Mrs. Fitzhugh sighed and followed. "She really is quite sane, Christie. It's just a phase she's going through. We've talked about getting her a puppy, but she'd probably be eating out of its bowl."

Christie couldn't believe Jenny's bedroom. Toys were scattered all over. It was the exact opposite of the rest of the house. Jenny's mother stood in the doorway and shook her head.

"We try to get her to be neat, but it's impossible. Jenny's got a mind of her own."

"Here, doggy," said Christie, picking up a doll. "Help me pick up some of these old bones."

Jenny bounded over to a stuffed toy and picked it up with her teeth. Carrying it to a large box under the window, she dropped it in and went after another.

As Mrs. Fitzhugh watched, Christie and Jenny put everything away. When they had finished, Jenny sat on the floor in front of Christie with her tongue hanging out, panting.

"Nice doggy." Christie patted her on the head.

"Well," said Mrs. Fitzhugh. "I must say, the method was a bit unusual, but that's the first time anyone has gotten her to put her things away. Would you be available to mind Jenny on Friday?"

"Sure," answered Christie.

"Very good. If you could be here by six-thirty, I'd appreciate it. That will give me time to show you the routine."

As they were talking, Jenny got up, took Christie's hand, and stood next to her. Christie squeezed it gently.

"How did it go?" Christie's mother asked when she returned home.

"Great. I got my first job as a child-minder. I'm going to mind Jenny for them Friday evening."

"Child-minder?" asked her father, smiling. "Is that anything like being a baby-sitter?"

"Don't tease," warned Mrs. Winchell.

Christie described what had happened at the Fitzhughs'. "Little Jenny's really cute. She's so lively, I don't think they know what to do with her."

"It sounds as if she needs someone young like you to be around," said her mother. "Your father and I were talking about the open house we're going to have. How does a week from Saturday sound to you, Christie?"

"Fine. Remember, Mum, I get to fill out the invitations."

"You can also deliver them for your *mum*," said Mr. Winchell, winking at his wife. Christie ignored him.

"You can invite some friends, too, if you'd like," said her mother.

Christie had just finished writing the last invitation when the phone rang, and her father called out that it was for her.

"Hi, Christie. This is Connie."

"Oh, hi, Connie." A thrill ran through Christie, but a little voice also said in her ear, "He's Nicki's."

"What have you been doing that's exciting?"

"Not much. I just finished filling out invitations to our open house."

"You're having an open house?"

Christie explained.

"Neat," he said. "Am I going to get an invitation?"

Caught off guard, Christie answered, "I'll have to see."

"While you're checking on that, why don't you check on whether you can go to the cinema with me Friday?"

"I've got a child-minding job Friday. I won't be going anywhere."

"Saturday then?" he persisted.

"I don't know."

"I don't think you like me. What's wrong? Do I have my head on backward?"

"Oh, no," she assured him quickly. "It's not that I don't like you. You're really nice."

"Then why won't you go out with me? Is it because of the fellow back home? You can't not date the rest of your life because of him. It's not normal."

"It's not just because of him," said Christie.

"Oh?"

She decided to tell him the truth. "Nicki McAfee likes you, and I don't want her to be mad at me."

"Ooh . . . that's why," he said, as if a great mystery had been cleared up. "Nicki is an all right bird, but we're not going regular together."

"That may be true, but I dated one of my best friend's boyfriends once when I thought they had broken up. It was a disaster," she told him, recalling how she had dated Keith Masterson. Even though Beth hadn't acted angry, Christie knew she had been hurt.

"Well, don't expect me to quit trying," he said cheerfully. "We Farrells aren't known for giving up when we've got the castle surrounded."

Christie had to laugh. She wished she could date him. He was fun. But if she did, and Nicki found out, it would be the end of any chance of their ever being friends.

CHAPTER

21

"Mind if I sit with you?" Phoebe asked as Christie took a seat on the bus the next morning. "Nicki's in a bit of a snit, and I don't want to be around her."

"What's wrong?" asked Christie.

"Oh, she thought his royal highness would call her for a date this weekend, and he hasn't. She's afraid he may be interested in someone else. Woe be unto whoever it is, if it's true."

Christie winced, "What makes Nicki so sarcastic?" she asked. "You said her brother's the same way."

"It's most likely because their parents don't pay much attention to them. Her mum and dad are always off on holiday to some exotic place. Nicki feels a bit like she's in the way." Phoebe pulled a book out of her knapsack and began to study.

155

Christie turned to look out the window. That explained a lot of things. It made her glad she had said no to Connie the night before. She took her hat off, and put it into her lap.

Wakeman Junior High was starting to seem so far away. When she'd looked at some of the yearbook pictures Jana had sent her, she'd realized that she hadn't even thought about some of the kids since leaving for London.

Christie glanced at her watch. Jana, Katie, Melanie, and Beth were all sound asleep in their beds at that very moment. They would wake up about the time she was eating lunch. Weird.

She wished she had friends like The Fabulous Five in England. The kids here liked her okay, but she wasn't really special to anyone. She glanced at the girl studying next to her. Perhaps Phoebe. That reminded Christie of something.

"Phoebe, my family's going to have an open house a week from Saturday so we can meet our neighbors. My mum said I can ask some friends. Would you like to come?"

"I'd love to," said Phoebe, closing her book. "I've been dying to see your flat. Count me in."

Just then the bus pulled up in front of St. Meg's, and they had to get off. I'll ask Eleanore, too, thought Christie. And maybe Nicki.

Christie caught Eleanore in the hallway that morning. The other girl seemed pleased when Christie invited her to the open house and said she would definitely be there.

By the time lunch hour came, the open house was starting to sound like fun. Christie wondered if she should ask Mrs. Mansfield to donate some of her flowers for decorations.

"I meant to tell you," Christie said to Phoebe as she took a seat at the dining table. "I got my first child-minding job. The Fitzhughs in our square asked me to watch their daughter Friday night."

"Oh, too bad it's Friday," replied Phoebe. "I was going to ask if you wanted to do something with Eleanore, Nicki, and me."

"Don't let them pay you below scale," chimed in Eleanore. "It'll hurt the rest of us."

"Yes, and make sure they have lots of soda and potato crisps for you to eat," added Becca, laughing.

"What we need is a good party," said Denise. "Everything is getting so boring. Hey, Nicki. Do you think you could talk Connie into having a party?"

"Your guess is as good as mine," replied Nicki gloomily. "He hasn't called me for a while."

"Maybe *you* ought to ask Connie, Christie," suggested Denise. "He called you for a date, didn't he?"

Christie blushed and glanced quickly at Nicki. "Just because he asked me for one date doesn't mean he's interested in me," she said, trying to divert the direction of the conversation. "Nicki knows him a lot better than I do. If anyone can get him to have a party, she can."

"Oh?" Becca raised her eyebrows. "Denise and I were talking to Charlie Fenwick, and he told us Connie is definitely interested in *you*."

Christie wished Becca hadn't said that. Nicki was practically crushing the slice of bread she was holding, and Christie could see sparks flying out of her eyes.

"Just because he called me once doesn't mean he's *that* interested in me."

"He didn't call you last night?" asked Denise. "Charlie said Connie was going to ring you up for a date this Friday."

Everyone's eyes were on Christie, and she felt trapped. Nicki was staring at her hard, waiting for her response.

"He did ring me up, but I told him no," said Christie firmly.

Nicki spoke up. "Did you talk to him before or after you got the child-minding job?"

Christie stared back at her. "After," she finally admitted softly.

Nicki tossed the piece of bread into her plate and angrily left the table.

After dinner that evening Christie went out to deliver the invitations. At the first three homes she put them in the mailbox. When she got to Mrs. Mansfield's, she rang the door bell instead.

"Well, what have we here?" asked Mrs. Mansfield. "You needn't have come all the way around to the front door, Christie. A rap on the back door would have been fine."

"I'm delivering invitations to the open house we're having, Mrs. Mansfield," said Christie. "And I wanted to thank you for telling the Fitzhughs about me."

"Well, come in for a moment and have some tea with me," said the old lady.

"I don't know if I should. I've got a lot of invitations to deliver."

"Of course you should," insisted Mrs. Mansfield, stepping back so Christie could enter. "I just finished baking, and the cake's still warm."

Mrs. Mansfield's flat was different from her family's and the Fitzhughs'. Instead of being neat, it was filled with odds and ends of furniture, most with scarves and afghans draped over their bulky arms and backs. The walls were filled with ornate framed pictures of what must have been Mrs. Mansfield's family. A sweet aroma filled the air.

Agatha, who had been sleeping on a sofa, saw Christie and jumped down to greet her.

Mr. Mansfield poured Christie some tea and cut her a huge piece of spice cake. It looked delicious.

"I wanted to tell you that the Fitzhughs called me," said Christie between bites. "They're going to use me Friday. And my mum loved the flowers you sent."

"Quite all right, dear. Now, tell me about your open house."

After Christie had shown her the invitation, Mrs.

Mansfield said, "Now, isn't that nice. I'd love to meet your lovely parents."

"I was wondering, Mrs. Mansfield. Could we maybe have some flowers from your garden to decorate?"

The old lady smiled. "Most certainly. Tell your mum I'll make up some bouquets and bring them over before."

Christie finished her cake and tea, scratched Agatha one more time, and left to deliver the rest of her invitations. Stopping at Mrs. Mansfield's had given her a warm feeling. It was like having a grandmother living just a few doors away.

The telephone was ringing when Christie walked back into her house. It was Nicki.

"Hi," said Christie nervously.

Nicki started right in. "Christie Winchell, I don't appreciate your leading Connie on when you know he and I have been dating."

"I haven't been leading him on," protested Christie. "I didn't encourage him to call me."

"You're certainly not *dis*couraging him, since he's still doing it. And it's no use trying to make it sound as if you turned him down for Friday night because you weren't interested, when the real reason was that you already had a child-minding job. I thought you wanted to be friends with me."

"I *do* want to be friends," said Christie.

"Well, you've got a funny way of showing it!"

The next thing Christie knew, the line was dead.

CHAPTER

22

Christie felt an icy chill coming from Nicki the entire next day. Once, when she passed Nicki and Phoebe walking together in the hall, Nicki stared straight ahead without even looking at Christie. Phoebe smiled and rolled her eyes sympathetically. Later, when Christie saw Phoebe in the hall by herself, she ran to catch up with her.

"Sorry about the way Nicki's acting," said Phoebe as Christie fell in step beside her. "She's got a big thing for Connie, you know, and she feels that you're competition."

"I can understand that," responded Christie. "But I wish she'd realize that I honestly don't intend to go out with Connie."

"Your not admitting up front that he called you made her suspicious."

"I know, but I was just trying to avoid exactly what's happened," said Christie. "I wanted to stay out of the middle of things between Connie and Nicki. I goofed."

"You can say that again," agreed Phoebe, chuckling.

"Forget about my going out with you guys, Friday night or *ever*," said Christie gloomily. "I've caused enough trouble already. I don't want Nicki to get angry at you, too."

"We'll see," Phoebe replied. "Nicki's got a temper, but she's really all right. I like her a lot, and I know you will, too, when you get to know her better."

When Christie got home after school, there was a large envelope waiting for her. The return address said "Katie Shannon" in big block letters. Giving her mother a quick kiss, Christie ran upstairs to her room and jumped into the middle of her bed. She opened the envelope and spilled out its contents.

Besides a letter, four booklets fell out. The first had "Beth Barry's Friendship Book" written on the front. The others said the same thing, except they had Melanie Edwards's, Katie Shannon's, and Jana Morgan's names on them. Each had a class picture of the author on the outside. Inside were places to put information—things she liked, things they had done together—and pictures. There was even a place to put her boyfriend's name and why she thought he was cute.

"Oh!" exclaimed Christie, as she turned the pages of Beth's book excitedly. "This is *terrific!*"

Christie picked up Katie's letter and read it.

Dear Christie:

Finally it was my turn to get a letter from you! Maybe I had the best turn of all, because I get to send you our friendship books and tell you some fantastic news.

The four of us saved our money, and we decided to call you at eleven o'clock in the morning Saturday after you get this letter. That should be four in the afternoon in London, right? Oh, PLEASE, PLEASE don't write back and tell us you won't be home to take the call! I can't tell you why, but it's important that we make the call then.

Boy, did we blow it. Beth told you in her letter how we were thinking about seeing if Alexis or Dekeisha would like to be part of our group. We did things with Alexis for a while first to see if it would work out with her. When she didn't seem interested, we asked Dekeisha to sit and go places with us. Then Alexis got mad, because she thought we didn't like her anymore. On top of that, Laura McCall started telling everyone that we were recruiting for The Fabulous Five. We finally saw how dumb we were acting. The Fabulous Five can only have the four of us and Christie Winchell in it, and that's the way it will always be. To prove it, we made up these friendship books for you. We made them for each other, too, We'd like you to make one about you for each of us.

I told Chase I was writing you a letter, and he said he was writing you one, too. I think he meant it.

Got to close for now. It makes me so happy to know we'll be talking to you next Saturday!
Love,
Katie

Tears welled up in Christie's eyes, and she pressed the letter to her chest. Katie was right. There could be only one Fabulous Five, and it *had* to have Katie, Jana, Beth, Melanie, and herself in it. If anyone of them weren't in the group, it wouldn't be *The Fabulous Five.*

When she thought about it, she realized she herself had been trying too hard to find substitutes for friends at home. There really wasn't another Jana or Katie or Melanie or Beth in the world, no matter how much some people might resemble them. Just the way I hoped deep down that there would never be another Christie for them, she thought. Why had it taken so long to figure that out?

Christie got her notebook and turned to some blank pages. She'd start that very moment to make friendship books for her friends.

She was still working on the books after dinner when the phone rang.

"Christie! It's for you!" her father called from downstairs.

She went to the study to answer.

"Hi, Christie. It's Connie."

Oh, no! thought Christie.

"Hi."

"I'm not calling for a date. I just want to talk—though I'm positive that if you get to know me better, you'll go out with me."

"Connie, I won't. Not as long as Nicki likes you."

"Nicki's nice, and I like her, but that doesn't mean I can't date someone else, does it?"

"No. But I don't like it that she's mad at me because of you, either."

"She's mad at you?"

Oops, thought Christie. She hadn't meant to let him know that.

"How did she know I was calling you, as if it were any of her business?"

Christie sighed. "Charlie Fenwick told Becca."

"Oh," he said slowly. "That Charlie needs to learn to curb his cake hole."

"To what?" asked Christie.

"Keep his mouth shut," said Connie.

They chatted a while longer, and after he had hung up, Christie went back to her room to finish her homework. Later she was taking her stuffed animals off her bed when the phone rang again, and her father called up the stairs.

"Hello."

"This is Nicki, Christie."

Christie braced herself for another tirade.

"I've just hung up from talking to Connie," said Nicki. "He told me that he asked you twice to go out with him."

Christie cringed.

"He also said you told him you wouldn't because of me." She sounded ashamed. "He said you didn't want to hurt me or have me angry at you. Connie said that had happened to you once before, and you didn't want it to happen again.

"I wish I had known that, Christie. But I guess I didn't give you a chance to tell me, did I? Here you were trying to be a friend, and I thought you were playing me for a fool. I guess I'm not a very trusting person. I feel like a blooming poop."

"It's okay, Nicki," Christie said softly.

"I want to be friends with you, Christie. Phoebe says you can't go out Friday with us, but what about Saturday? Maybe together we can talk Connie into having a party."

Christie laughed. "That sounds like fun. And, Nicki, my family is having an open house a week from Saturday. Can you come?"

CHAPTER

23

"Would you look at the crowd?" exclaimed Beth as she glanced around Bumpers. The fast-food restaurant was packed with kids who had come to be in on the telephone call with Christie.

Heather Clark, Marcie Bee, and Sara Sawyer were talking to Richie Corrierro and Brian Olsen by the Wurlitzer jukebox. Mona Vaughn and Matt Zeboski were sitting in a bright yellow carnival bumper car, and Dekeisha and Marcie were talking to Don Petry and Derek Travelstead. Even Funny Hawthorne had come—without the rest of The Fantastic Foursome. Chase was sitting at a table near the cash register with Keith, Shane, Tony, and Randy. Other kids wandered around or sat in booths or bumper cars, talking.

"Wow!" exclaimed Melanie. "I can only dream that

this many kids would want to talk to me if I moved away. I'm glad we didn't wait until this afternoon. Too many kids were going to be doing other things."

"Did you bring the speaker phone and the money, Katie?" asked Jana. "It's a quarter to eleven. We need to get set up."

"Got both right here in my backpack," responded Katie, patting her bag.

Mr. Matson was all smiles when they approached him. "Since this phone call has increased my Saturday morning business by at least a thousand percent, I'm going to contribute ten dollars to help pay for the call," he said jovially.

"That's great, Mr. Matson," cheered Melanie, bouncing up and down. "Quick, Katie, figure out how much longer we can talk."

"You do it while I get the phone plugged in and tested," said Katie.

"While you two are doing that, Beth and I'll get everyone organized," said Jana. She and Beth positioned themselves in front of the jukebox.

"LISTEN UP, EVERYBODY!" Beth tried to shout over the noise of everyone's talking.

Chase saw what they were trying to do, and he put two fingers in his mouth and let out a piercing whistle. That got everyone's attention.

"All right," said Jana, looking at her watch. "In about ten minutes we're going to place the call to Christie. When we've got her on the line, The Fabulous Five will say hello first, then we'll put her on the

speaker so everybody can hear and she can hear you.
When I give the signal, everybody yell '*Hellooo, Christie!*' Then line up by the phone and you can say hello
to her again. Now let's practice. Okay . . . *say it*!" she
ordered the crowd.

"Hellooo, Christie!" they yelled.

"Not good enough! LET'S HEAR IT!" she
shouted, waving her hands.

"*HELLOOO, CHRISTIE!*" they screamed.

"ALL RIGHT!" Beth yelled, throwing up her fists.

"We'll have her on the line in about five minutes," Jana
said, checking her watch again. "Everybody be ready.

Christie picked Jenny up and put her on her hip.
"You've got to stay out from under people's feet,
sweetie," she said, brushing the little girl's hair out of
her eyes.

"How come she thinks she's a dog?" asked Phoebe.
"Does it run in her family?"

Christie laughed and looked at her watch. The open
house had turned out to be a lot of fun, especially since
Phoebe, Nicki, Eleanore, and even Connie had come
over. Nearly all their neighbors were there, too. Mrs.
Mansfield's flowers looked gorgeous as centerpieces on
the tables, and her father had fires going in both fireplaces. But what made Christie most excited was the
fact that it was five minutes until four. The Fabulous
Five would be calling any minute. She was so eager to
talk to them, she could hardly stand it.

"Her mother and father say it's just a phase Jenny's going through," said Christie, answering Phoebe's question. "I think it's her way of pretending she has a dog to play with. When I minded her last Friday, we had lots of fun, and she didn't play like she was a doggy once. I'm going to work on Mr. and Mrs. Fitzhugh and see if I can't talk them into getting Jenny a pet of some kind."

Connie interrupted their conversation to change the subject. "Well, I talked my mum into letting me have the party you girls have been all over me about. But since it's your idea, Nicki and Christie, you've got to help me carry it off."

"Well, in that case, I think we should have the food brought in by the queen's own caterer," Nicki told him. "Do it up right, you know."

"If we do that, it'll come out of my allowance," said Connie. "I'd be broke for the next zillion years."

"Well, aren't your friends worth it?" asked Eleanore.

"Not *my* friends," responded Connie, laughing.

Christie listened to her new friends kidding each other. They *are* my friends, she thought. And so are some of the other kids at school. I'm finally starting to fit in.

And then there was the wonderful Mrs. Mansfield, and the Fitzhughs, and her teacher, Miss Woolsey. They all like me. London didn't feel totally like home yet, but she was starting to like it a lot better. If only The Fabulous Five were here, things would be *almost* perfect. The only other missing person would be Chase.

Christie hoisted Jenny a little higher and looked at her new friends. The Fabulous Five would like them, she told herself. I think they'd like them very much.

"Telephone, honey." Christie was surprised by her father's announcement. She hadn't heard the phone ring.

"It's your friends," said Phoebe. "We'll wait down here so you can talk to them in private."

"No." Christie grabbed her hand. "I want you all to come up to the study with me."

"Hello! Christie! Is that really you? *It's really her! It's really her!*" Katie cried to the kids huddled around her.

"It's me, Katie. How are you? You're fine? Great. Let me put Melanie on, Christie, before she rips the phone out of my hand. I'll be back."

Chase, Randy, Tony, Shane, and Keith had left their seats to be closer to the phone. Other kids were beginning to crowd in behind them.

"Christie, this is Melanie. It is really you? Did you get the friendship books we sent you? Great. I miss you. Do you miss me? I really wish you were here, Christie. Beth wants to talk to you, but don't you dare hang up without talking to me again. Promise?"

"Hi, Christie. I miss you, too." Chase reached for the phone, and Beth pushed his hand away. "Things aren't the same without you, Christie. You what? You met a cat named Agatha? I can't believe it. I'll have to tell our Agatha. Mom, Dad, Brian, Todd, Brittany, and Alicia said to tell you hello. Jana wants the phone now. I'll talk to you again, too."

"Hi, Christie, this is Jana. How come we're all passing the phone so fast?" Jana pushed back at the kids who were pressing in on her. "Because we've got a fantastic surprise for you. Hold on and listen real closely."

Jana punched the speaker button on the phone and pointed at the kids.

"*HELLOOO, CHRISTIE! WE MISS YOU!*" they all screamed at the tops of their lungs.

Christie's voice came over the speaker. "*What? Who's there? Who is that?*"

"Me for one," said Mr. Matson, leaning over so he could speak into the phone. "This is Mr. Matson, Christie. My place is filled with your friends. You wouldn't believe the crowd."

"This is Chase, Christie. I wrote you a letter. Promise to write back."

"I promise," said Christie, her voice quivering.

One after another the kids filed by the telephone to say hello to Christie.

"I miss you, too, Dekeisha," said Christie. Dekeisha had to be about the one hundredth person from Wacko Junior High Christie had talked to. Tears were streaming down her face as Phoebe and the others watched, and Jenny ran her fingers through the dampness on Christie's cheeks. Christie didn't care.

"Jana, is that you again? How'd you do this?" asked Christie as her friend's voice came over the phone. "It's amazing, and I love you guys for it."

"Mr. Matson let us put a speaker phone by his cash register. He's even chipping in on the cost of the call."

"Are Katie, Beth, and Melanie right by you?" asked Christie.

"Yes."

"Good. I want you guys to hear something, too." Christie turned to her friends in the room. "Say, 'Hello, Fabulous Five,' as loud as you can," she directed, holding the phone out so the kids in the study could speak into it.

"*HELLO, FABULOUS FIVE!*" they all yelled.

"Hewo, Faboowas Five!" said Jenny.

"Jana?"

"Yes, Christie. I'm right here."

"Could I maybe talk to Chase for a minute without the speaker on?"

"Sure," said Jana. "Let me get him back."

Phoebe took Jenny from Christie and shooed the others out of the room.

"Christie?"

Chase's voice made Christie feel good all over. "Yes," she said softly.

Christie stacked her bears around her when she went to bed that night. She missed The Fabulous Five terribly, but her friends in London were awfully nice, too. It was like knowing two worlds instead of one. The two were different, but each was special in its own way. When her family moved back to the United States in a few years, she would probably have as hard a time leaving these people as she had had leaving The Fabulous Five. Especially little Jenny.

Christie sighed and pulled her bears in around her. It was nice having a home on both sides of the ocean.

Katie sat on her bed and stroked her yellow cat, Libber. She smiled to herself. The day had been great. She had been scared when some of the kids, like Richie, wouldn't let go of the phone, and they started going over their half hour. As it turned out, with Mr. Matson putting in his ten dollars, they had two dollars and fifty cents left over. The Fabulous Five had decided to save it for their next call to Christie.

For Katie, talking to Christie had been like being released from some kind of hold. Now Katie could imagine Christie in her new home with her new friends, and everything was all right. Christie seemed safe and happy, and that was good.

The boy named Connie had been at Christie's when they talked to her. Melanie wondered if Chase had noticed, and if he had, she wondered what had gone through his mind.

Connie's family is royalty, Melanie thought. I may never meet royalty in my whole life, and Christie already has. But that's okay. If one of The Fabulous Five had to move, it was probably best that it was Christie.

She's proved how easily she can handle it. I know I would have spent all my time thinking about my friends back home. Christie didn't. She just went out and made friends. Melanie pulled out her friendship books and started looking through them.

"Wow, what a scene," Beth said, as she scratched her Old English sheepdog, Agatha, behind the ears. Beth was lying on her bed with Agatha at her side.

"I'd sure like to visit Christie in London sometime, Agatha. I wonder if Melanie's father could win another contest and take us all on vacation there, like when we went to Barbados. Wouldn't it be something if you could go along and meet Agatha the cat? You'd make friends with her, wouldn't you Agatha?"

Agatha took a deep breath and let out a sigh, as if she couldn't care less.

"Well, maybe you wouldn't like to go," continued Beth, "but I would. Some day I'd like to travel all over the world, like Christie. Now that she's done it, I want to, too. Maybe one of these days," said Beth, running her fingers through the dog's fur.

Jana sat by her window and looked out. If her eyes were only good enough to see London. She chuckled to herself. It had been funny the way Christie had had those other kids in her room say hello over the phone. Jana thought they had sounded like fun kids, too. She was glad. It would be terrible to imagine Christie all alone. Jana looked at her watch. Christie had probably just tucked herself into bed.

Jana went over and opened her window and looked in the direction she thought London was. Sticking her head out, she took a deep breath and then whispered: *"Good night, Christie."*

Watch for the next book about The Fabulous Five, *Laura's Secret*, coming to your bookstore soon. Here's a scene from that book:

Laura McCall removed the last of the dishes from the dishwasher. Next she went to the pantry and got out the iron and ironing board. She wished her father would learn to press his own darn shirts. She was tired of having to do them for him when he forgot to send one to the cleaners. She had enough to do. And he had the nerve to call her his chief cook and bottle washer.

Of course none of her friends—not even the rest of The Fantastic Foursome—knew how much work she had at home. They all thought she had it made, living with her swinging bachelor father, who drove a red Maserati. She smiled to herself. And that's *exactly* what I want them to think.

But if they only knew what it was really like, she thought. Especially not having a mother to go to for advice and help when she needed it. It hadn't mattered so much when she was younger, but now that she was thirteen, she had a lot of questions, and no one to ask but her father. And he was no help at all.

She sighed as she tested the iron and spread the shirt on the board. Well, she was certainly not going to let anyone know what her life was really like, especially The Fantastic Foursome. If they ever found out, she would just die.

* * *

What Laura doesn't know is that something is about to happen that *will* let her friends see what actually goes on in her home. When she tries to cover up her secret by telling one little lie, that lie suddenly snowballs, and everything gets out of control. Find out how Laura deals with her problem in The Fabulous Five #26: *Laura's Secret*, coming to your bookstore soon.

FABULOUS FACTS ABOUT THE FABULOUS FIVE

Do you and your friends know the answers to these trivia questions about The Fabulous Five? Quiz each other to see who knows the most Fabulous Facts!

1. In The Fabulous Five Super #1, *The Fabulous Five in Trouble*, what unbelievable thing happens to the girls at a sleepover at Katie's house?

2. In book #2, *The Trouble with Flirting*, what are the seven tips for flirting that Melanie finds in a magazine?

3. In book #16, *The Hot-Line Emergency*, whom does Christie suspect of being the mysterious caller?

4. In book #12, *Katie's Dating Tips*, why does the science teacher, Mr. Dracovitch, come to school dressed as Dracula?

5. In book #4, *Her Honor, Katie Shannon*, why does Katie get a detention?

You can find the answers to these questions, plus five more questions about Fabulous Facts, in the back of The Fabulous Five #26, *Laura's Secret*, coming to your bookstore soon!

ABOUT THE AUTHOR

Betsy Haynes, the daughter of a former news-woman, began scribbling poetry and short stories as soon as she learned to write. A serious writing career, however, had to wait until after her marriage and the arrival of her two children. But that early practice must have paid off, for within three months Mrs. Haynes had sold her first story. In addition to a number of magazine short stories and the Taffy Sinclair series, Mrs. Haynes is also the author of *The Great Mom Swap* and its sequel, *The Great Boyfriend Trap*. She lives in Marco Island, Florida, with her husband, who is also an author.

Taffy Sinclair is perfectly gorgeous and totally stuck-up. Ask her rival Jana Morgan or anyone else in the sixth grade of Mark Twain Elementary. Once you meet Taffy, life will **never** be the same.

Don't Miss Any of the Terrific Taffy Sinclair Titles from Betsy Haynes!

Follow the adventures of Jana and the rest of **THE FABULOUS FIVE** in a new series by Betsy Haynes.